COVID-26
Zombie

Roger Schafer

Dedication

This story is dedicated to my family: to my mother, Barbara Schafer, my father, Roger Schafer, and my brothers, Michael and Danny Schafer.

I also would like to thank everyone involved in this project and hope you all enjoy the next adventures of Eko and Indra.

Acknowledgment

A lot of people believe that there is nothing you can do alone, and you always need the support of someone else around you to help you achieve something. The case with me is similar. A lot of people played a part in assisting me with the completion of this book and with this section, I would like to extend my gratitude to them.

About the Author

Roger "Derby" Schafer was born in New Mexico and has lived in Las Vegas, Nevada, most of his adult life. In the past, he played and coached numerous sports. As a Coach in Roller Hockey, his Team Won Nationals once and often had top teams competing on National Level for many years. He is the oldest of the three children in his family, all of who reside in Las Vegas, Nevada.

Preface

2020, the COVID-19 A.K.A. "Coronavirus" began and became newsworthy during the early part of that year. This was the beginning of a shift for mankind worldwide. COVID/Corona was the start that created change affecting everyone's life in every way imaginable.

These citizens were losing their rights which happened with little to no resistance. When citizens lost their rights, governments worldwide were in total control and used the media to keep that control. Media and the government demanded these changes, which in effect gave complete control to all civilized countries and their governments. Immediate changes impacted and forced businesses, schools, and most of the Private Sector to close unless they were deemed "essential" services by all governments worldwide.

Never before in all of our written history have privately owned businesses been told to cease all operations by the government, worldwide. Life before COVID/Corona was to be no more. Life now, with Corona, and in the future is the "new normal." Many will even consider these the best of times. "Personal Protection Equipment (PPE)" requirements would change to "lawfully required" in most cities worldwide, and "Social Distancing" enforced. COVID-19's presence became common knowledge in 2020, yet we were foolish enough to believe that it would be over as the year came to an end. 2021 was about to begin and even as death rates would continue to decrease, it was not being reported. The media, which is controlled and regulated by the government, decide what is newsworthy. Along with current/former Government officials, media in all major countries would do as they have been instructed... instructed.

Those who control the choices and dictate what will or needs to happen are known as "The One Percent." They are an exclusive group of people, who have net worths in trillions of dollars. When 'The 1%' combine their efforts, they have enough power to control almost any government worldwide. High-ranking government officials answer to the 1% due to the power they possess by running the corporate world. If the same government officials do not comply with their demands, they will be replaced or removed. This new Society has been split up into two main groups.

The first group is known as "The Sheep." They are gullible followers of the news, media, and government. They have been tricked into being terrified of COVID-19 and all other types of viruses/illnesses. They will follow all of the government's COVID-19 rules and regulations without opposition.

On the other hand, there are "The Wolves." Those who do not trust what the media tells them to believe. They do not support what the government has become since the start of COVID-19 either. The Wolves want to keep their personal rights and freedoms and are the only voice of the opposition.

At the start of COVID-19, the Public was given a set of guidelines to follow on how to protect themselves against the virus. They would eventually need to learn and understand these guidelines on self-protection because of what was to come shortly after the start of COVID. This required protection would be the beginning of a curse that would do far greater harm than the virus was capable of. No one knew how dangerous it was to wear the mask and face shields until it was too late. The guidelines set for self-protection were a mistake; one that would curse all of humanity. Humans were about to transform.

The first transformation began with the lower tier of humans, now known as the "Z." Shortly after the Zs were discovered, another species was found. This species was definitely superior to the Z population and would be called "Zombies." The social requirements put in place for self-protection created both the Z and the Zombie population. This is what most humans feared would happen if they complied. They knew something bad was to come of this. COVID-19 would kill seven people out of every hundred thousand. The Z and the Zombies could kill billions more leaving humankind fearing possible extinction.

The COVID-26 Zombies and the Z would change the entire world forever. Those who wish to survive and stop the extinction of humankind would need help. The Wolves were needed now more than ever.

Contents

Page Left Blank Intentionally

Chapter 1
The Year 2020

The control room was absolutely still but buzzing, but not with noise, with worries – every single mind had them. The crew could see it in the glances they gave to each other or avoided, the adjusting of collars, and the clearing and gulping of throats. The graphics team, editors, the teleprompter operator, and production assistants, even the director, felt too reserved to say anything. They had their eyes glued to the reporters.

In the news agency, there was no rest for the wicked; all of their lives were on the line. But things, as they knew, were changing. The new SOPs demanded a distance of two chairs between attendants, hand sanitizers mounted on the walls, and masks on their faces. This arrangement would have seemed alien to the crew a month ago, but this was the new protocol; the new norm. The final countdown was announced, the broadcast began, yet the studio still sat as glum as it was minutes ago.

"The virus outbreak in question, now termed as a global pandemic, grew as a threat in December of 2019. At present, it continues to grow more potent by the day. We remind our viewers that it was discovered when the World Health Organization studied several pneumonia cases of unknown origin in Wuhan City, in the Hubei Province of China. What could have been a common cold turned out to be something deadly," the male reporter presented, trying to enunciate clearly and with inflections. It seemed to demand an effort to do what was routine.

Then it was the cue for the female reporter, who sullenly took over. "On January 7th," she began, "Chinese authorities identified the cause of alleged pneumonia to be a novel strain of the coronavirus, which, as you must now be aware is a member of the family of viruses that have never been encountered before. The authorities have termed it as CoVid-19…"

Far away from the news agency, a young straight couple walked on the empty Maple Street, hands in their pockets, and constantly on the lookout so nobody would see them violate quarantine rules.

"Can we kiss? I'll be real quick," the man asked restlessly through his surgical mask.

"NO. We cannot risk it, not even holding hands." Those were two valid reasons, but she had a third. The distance between them was enough to fit at least two obese people. And this was the new norm now.

The girl was fidgeting, having researched the fate-altering virus all day. The boy knew this.

"Hey," he asked. "Why don't you tell me about this virus? Why is it called that? COVID-19 and… Yeah? What's with it?" *Is it really all that serious*? he also wanted to ask. But he knew that he should not.

"It's simple," she said nonchalantly. "This Virus is called COVID-19 because 'Co' stands for 'Corona,' 'Vi' stands for 'Virus,' and 'D' stands for 'Disease.' 2019 is the year of origin, so 19."

"Cool."

That's when she disclosed to him that she cannot carry on meeting him like this and that the virus is making her want to break up…

In another building nearby, a magazine reporter was conducting an interview with a renowned clinician in town.

"So, it looks like the more common human coronaviruses have been diverse, but largely more mild, yeah?" the interviewer's voice was muffled by the mask on his face.

"Uh-huh," the doctor sitting on a sofa on the other end of the room said, shifting his legs. "The more common ones have been known to cause benign to moderate upper-respiratory tract illnesses. Umm… these tend to be like the common cold and all, you know, with symptoms that don't last for long. May I fetch you some tea, by the way, I totally forgot to ask earlier."

The reporter's eyes bulged as he looked up. He immediately recovered with a smile. "No, I'm good. I got a water bottle in my bag. Would you please continue?"

"I know, I know. It's risky, but everything in my kitchen is sterilized. But anyway, as I was saying. There have been two known human coronaviruses, MERS-CoV and SARS-CoV, that have been known to cause severe symptoms, and even death."

The journalist recorded the notes quickly, without pausing his audio recording. "And what are your predictions about the cure, doctor?"

"Well, the world of medicine has seen its share of miracle cures. We have treated almost every threat from the polio vaccine to heart transplants." Then, he inched closer to the reporter. "But let me tell you this, journalist, these past achievements may pale in comparison IF we could find a cure for this bastard. It's showing signs of resilience the likes of which the best of the best medical practitioners have never seen."

The magazine reporter's hand froze. He looked up, and the light-hearted doctor could only give him a sympathetic shrug. "My age has already come. It's up to your generation Z to deal with the deadliest virus in the history of man."

***

The talk of the COVID-19 pandemic had gone viral worldwide, no pun intended. All conversations included what the media was saying about this uncontrollable pandemic. Friends who had no interest in medicine constantly kept each other in the loop. Some started activist movements about research on antidotes and awareness campaigns. "Wokeness" held a new meaning now, catalyzed by the Coronavirus.

Old people all over the world were most vulnerable to contracting the disease. The doctors told them it was due to their weakening immune systems. The young ones watched with tears in their eyes as ambulances came and carried their grandparents or older uncles and aunts away.

Parents could no longer hug their children out of fear. They could not have known that what their elders were describing as a loss of smell and taste, then a fever, would be followed by severe illness. They would require respirators to aid in their recovery, while the hospitals were running out of them.

The media broadcasts kept blasting non-stop, focusing on this never-before-seen strain of Coronavirus in humans. For months, the hot topic remained ahead of all other issues. It was everywhere, all over television, the internet, talk shows, and even the radio. Only a media detox and going AWOL helped the people stay away from the waves of anxiety that was spreading. When confronted, "Ignorance is bliss," would be their response.

ROGER SCHAFER

Talk began to spread throughout global gatherings such
as places of worship (churches, mosques, temples), schools,
hospitals, and the workplace for most. What started as
precautionary measures for a preventative cure, now looked
like the hope of a better solution.

And this was felt everywhere. In the US, the wisest minds
were gathering for primetime talk shows, debating the best
non-medical and social intervention that the governments
could legislate until the cure came out. "It's high time that
our leaders do something. We can't just sit and watch
America go through something like Italy underwent. We
can't afford 900 people dying daily…"

Naturally, the media kept flooding people with all the
information they had on the Coronavirus. Sometimes, this
would include the very misinformed perspectives too. But
eventually, the collective voice and demands grew
tremendous enough to confront the politicians of the world.
Most of them would not have prodded to action if it wasn't
for the public.

World leaders and government officials forcefully pushed
and backed the need for immediate, efficient solutions. Some
of them were too late in their responses, while others avidly

fired back. "COVID-19 could without a doubt create the highest future mortality rate known to the World if we don't take action," leaders like the Prime Minister of New Zealand claimed.

The media continued to keep the masses and the governments in check while the moroseness within their agencies continued. With its accountability-seeking methods, the news and public awareness became the cause of headaches for several ministers, Congressmen, and Congresswomen. They would be seen fumbling in interviews and pulling out sheets upon sheets of facts that they themselves could not understand.

Some downplayed it, but others considered the virus seriously for what it was. Some government officials partnered with their media outlets to ensure that people knew millions, possibly even billions, could die due to the deadly Coronavirus. The news had spread like wildfire in every language that the virus will forever affect the present and the future. Antagonizing was the fact that with all the modern technology, not the most qualified medical experts could produce a breakthrough with the vaccine.

Acknowledging that there was no dodging reorganization at the mass scale to contain the virus, an unprecedented step was taken right where the virus had begun.

The conference table at the Chinese office was set with all standard operating procedures, equipped with masks, and everyone being aware of social distancing. Next to every government official sat a generous bottle of hand sanitizer, too. At the beginning of the conference, there was a fever check to ensure the meeting was safe. Luckily for the President, all his representatives were free of the disease.

But nobody was focused on that concern for now. Not momentarily. Especially since the instructions that were in their hands were revolutionary. It made many absentmindedly grasp the cup of water placed opposite to the sanitizer. Concerns and questions at the table were veritably voiced, just as the President had expected.

"The businesses would suffer…"

"What about the economy?"

"Do you realize the healthy people will be at risk when enclosed with the infected ones indoors…?"

The President listened to each of the questions and presented his arguments calmly. Everyone was convinced by the end that this was the best possible solution under the circumstances. The news reached the Wuhan officials of the lockdown, in folders filled with heavy and well-researched guidelines. It was to be effective immediately there.

The lockdown measures were commendable, extending first to the nearby cities of Huanggang and Ezhou, then were adopted by almost all the countries in the world.

The US was no exception to this. The American media, led by its President, who was initially denying the severity of the virus, was straightened by the public and his high-ranking government officials such as senators and members of Congress. They all instilled fear into the general public, so much so that the demands for a country-wide lockdown were hyped and imposed.

The inception of the coronavirus pandemic had broken out when the Presidential Elections in the United States of America were to set afoot. Before the 'COVID,' Franklin Fowler, a Republican candidate, and the United States' President was winning the presidential election.

The Democrats, being the opposing party, did not have any strong points to help them run against the President, nor did they have what they needed for the Democratic Party to gain the lead in this Year's election. Democrats and even some members of the Republican party who greatly opposed Franklin Fowler had needed something to change the narrative to win the 2020 Presidential Election. The Coronavirus became just that reason.

The stout and overconfident figure, known for his audacious brown head of hair, was running for his second controversial term in the Office. "I'm a man with many powerful friends and enemies both, I cannot fear the midgets," he said to his secretary when she cautioned him about the backlash the public was giving him. He was incompetent and had retaliated with a lockdown response to Covid-19 too late. The statistics in the nation looked ugly, terrifyingly worse than those of Italy.

His incompetence was not the only reason why many government officials such as "Congress-Senators" hated Fowler. It was also to secure the timeless game of power. Fowler was not wrong about his enemies, which included opposing officials in other countries other than his own.

None of them wanted Fowler to succeed with his efforts. But little did they know, Fowler had at his back immense support.

"Whose support does Fowler have?" one of three teenage friends interested in propaganda and scandals asked. The rest were gathered at his place, watching the news.

His friend replied, "Allow me to explain. It's not quite the chicken and egg question, but not many consciously think about this: so we know that the government controls the Media, right?"

Everybody nodded.

"Yet, do you wonder who controls the government? I'll spare the dramatics and just reveal. The answer is the rich one percent, guys. Those at the top. They control it all."

The other friend claps his hand in recollection. "The one percent exactly," he proclaimed, "they are the top one percent of the richest of people. And we're not just talking about the US, but one percent from all around the world. They harness enough power and social status to control entire governments in each and every country."

Indeed, when the virus first began, one percent of the world saw it as a golden opportunity to ensure greater wealth, power, and social status. Even more importantly, it was the perfect time to gain the world domination they always craved for. That, along with the segregation of social classes so that only 2 classes of all humans remained worldwide.

The one percent were a class of their own, and the other 99 percent made up the rest. When this happened, which they proposed inevitably will, even millionaires and billionaires were at the same level as the other ninety-nine percent.

January 2020: the yellow-hat wearing scientist entered the cave after excavating his surroundings. It was dripping in places, but for the past 7 days, he had been getting used to the cave. A rumor had been ongoing that the virus sample he and his partner found in Wuhan was owed to a live animal market that was not following proper handling guidelines. He wanted to see how his partner would react to the news.

"That was just a rumor though," his partner responded absently, focused on his sample. Then he turned around to his partner, "and I might just actually know what the truth could be," he said to the first.

"Really?" his partner responded, his mask muffling his voice.

"Yeah. The results for the sample we gathered with our latest equipment invented for the ISEF competition… it's out," he said dejectedly, but his face maintained its stoic.

"What is it? Why won't you tell?"

"This virus has originated in China, but not in the way you and I might have been speculating. It didn't just come into being due to some weird mixture of chemicals and animals or whatever. This virus, it was created…probably in some secret super lab that for all we know must have been guarded by the military."

His friend's jaw dropped upon hearing that. Sweat beaded on his forehead that had now dampened his surgical mask.

"And also, for all I know, we may be the only two people who know about this."

Their mobile phone mics had heard exactly what they said. Within a minute, the circuitry within was activated, and an explosive went off. It was potent enough to kill both scientists.

Chapter 2
The Virus

The boy in the hoodie was skeptical and wary on the inside, but he did not show it. He was following an armed stranger in a slim alley. It stank of gutters and dead mice. This is how everything smelled these days, so that did not worry him.

What made him anxious was the empty eeriness of the alley. Everything around him was a musty brown, even the metallic shutters with black paint. The wind whistled only to carry dust or make shattered windows clap.

"How much farther now?" the boy asked, taking a deep breath. He wondered if his voice was loud enough.

His guide, a dark, lean man with blue and green dreads, told him they were almost there. He did not turn around, but the magazine of his Bersa pistol seemed to constantly be on the kid. The man had told the boy at the start not to worry about the weapon. Since then, the boy could not help but worry about the weapon.

They skipped one final puddle before the man with the dreads bent down at a shutter. He pulled a key out from his pockets and fit it into a lock. In a few seconds, the shutters went up. The man entered the blackness without a backward glance. The kid only kept staring with clenched fists.

"Come inside. We can't risk being seen."

The boy came inside, the shutters went down, and a screen lit up before him; a projector screen, he discovered.

The man with the dreadlocks was gone now. A light-skinned woman in a green tank top and dirty sneakers stood facing him instead. She was semi-lit, only by the screen. Matthew could see the tattoo on her bare arm. "Don't ask for my name. I'll be your host for the initiation. Please be seated, Matthew."

Matthew wiped the sweat on his face and took one of the many seats facing the screen. It felt good to be called by his name after so long.

"You might be aware of some of the things you will watch and hear now. Many other things might be difficult to swallow. Or not. Depending on… well, just how you are."

The woman had a young face, but it did not radiate youth. Matthew was not sure if he and his old friends would have called this one pretty. She continued saying, "Just keep your mind open. And at least try to relax."

I am relaxed, Matthew wanted to say, but he just realized his knees were shaking. He made them stop and eased into the chair. Matthew was ready.

A man in glasses and a lab coat appeared on the screen. He began without any introductions or salutations.

"To understand how COVID-19 was the beginning of a master plan made by a few elites that resulted in the creation of what our generation knows as COVID-Z or the Zombie virus, let me take you back to the late twentieth century. We will trace the history of the many viruses the world has seen.

In 1976, the outbreak of Ebola had started in the Democratic Republic of Congo. It was a unique virus that affected people who exchanged bodily fluids such as vomit, blood, semen, etc. Soon after, AIDS (Acquired Immune Deficiency Syndrome), too followed, also transferred through bodily fluids. This started to become known as the deadliest disease in the world.

Mad Cow Disease began in the latter part of the 1990s as another life-threatening disease. This virus struck only before the bug called Y2K, standing for the Year 2000. The Y2K was supposed to be the end of electricity and all modern technology. People thought after that happened, the world would come to an end. It, of course, did not.

After that, something really revolutionary boiled in the minds of a few. The deadliest virus of its time, SARS (Severe Acute Respiratory Syndrome), struck in 2002. Yes, SARS overtook the hype that AIDS had promulgated. This was believed to have originated in China, much like the beloved COVID-19.

If you were there at the time, your parents might have told you that COVID-19 Virus was basically a stronger version of 'SARS.' If not, well, at least now you know.

So, the entire media became obsessed with SARS. So much fear-mongering occurred that they would broadcast, print, or even place only SARS-related news throughout the media and internet. But before the SARS could catch the summit of its hype, an intervention occurred.

It was the day of September 11, 2001. On that day, America was attacked by terrorists. The kamikaze pilots successfully brought down both World Trade Center buildings by crashing commercial airplanes into them. Thousands of people died, and the iconic twin towers in New York were obliterated.

Most of the Americans were more concerned with terrorism than fearing a virus. Even the media knew this, and SARS quickly became a thing of the past. It simply could not compete against the terrorism and the day of September 11, 2001.

Later in the late 2000s, the next big thing was Swine Flu. The 2009 swine flu outbreak originated in Veracruz, Mexico. Health workers traced the virus to a pig farm in this southeastern Mexican state. A young boy who lived nearby was among the first people to contract the swine flu.

As it had happened in the past, the swine flu was another tool to ensure that the media could go back to the fear tactic. It helped the US media that the outbreak dissipated from a country directly connected with the southern part of the United States of America.

Next to happen was another broadcasted and feared event known as the H5N1 Bird Flu virus. Like all the other viruses before the H5N1 Bird Flu, this was predicted to be a worldwide killer of a large percentage of the population.

Yet, most of the people belonging to the population of that time, survived, including me. It shouldn't come as a surprise that very few actually died, based on the world's population. The same was the case for all the population-exterminating viruses mentioned above.

One fact that is not often discussed is that across the globe, an average of 160,000 people died on a single day in the 2010 decade. That is approximately 5 million people per month and an average of 57 million people per year.

The media, controlled by the government and the government, controlled by the 1%, knew that to be successful, it would require the use of a very powerful tool, FEAR. And that too, in the general population. Given our history and the way it turned out, fear has been the only thing that did change the narrative. It is fear that has created many problems in our world, way more deadly than all the COVIDs.

Back to the topic of COVID-19, as of July 2020, somewhere around 12 million Coronavirus cases had been reported across 188 countries and territories. There were around 580,000 deaths. More than 6.5 million people had recovered. We are talking about a time where 7.9 billion people were living."

The man on the screen moved to a chalkboard now.

"Let us conduct simple math of 580,000 people worldwide who died or were reported dead due to Coronavirus. Let us divide the deaths by the population of 7.9 Billion." The man expertly carried out the calculation on the board before coming up with the result. "Ah, that breaks down to 0.0000734225% of the world's population dying.

To break it down in easier terms, 0.0000734225% means that 7 out of 100,000 people had died due to Coronavirus. The news was not interested in provided figures such as these and informing the public that the death rate had continued to decline worldwide. Instead, the focus was on the number of positive tests showing up, made possible because more people were being tested.

Additionally, those who tested positive and took another positive test were counted as two cases, even though it was one person. Quite often, certain groups of people would be tested frequently.

This happened at the global scale, so to know the factual amounts would require only guessing, not the scientific, statistical date the media was showing.

Positive tests even occurred when a person who had the virus, at an earlier point, yet were not ill at the time of testing. This situation would officially be recorded as Infected, even though they were no longer ill. Each time this group was tested, even if hundreds of times and even if by a single person, it would be classified as New Infections.

Not to mention that at the minimum, 17% of the tests would produce inaccurate results. Even if a person was not positive, a faulty test could show them positive and infected. Now, of course, the other side to that is someone who may actually be sick and infected with a negative result would not be put in the correct category as being Positive based on faulty testing.

These were the factors not at all discussed nor mentioned but were happening. This turned up the Fear knob, and very few stood up during those times to question or even challenge what the media and experts were telling us to do. Many were lying low behind the scenes too. They did not follow any of the requirements of Personal Protection Equipment (PPE), which included face masks, gloves, and/or hand sanitizer or social distancing.

At first, PPE and social distancing were only "suggested" things. But of course, it was shortly after the "suggestion" phase that these became requirements. It started becoming enforced by law enforcement too. Businesses that did not comply would be fined and even shut down. The clients who did not follow the guidelines would be mocked and sanctioned too.

In some parts of the US and around the world, many of those who did not comply with the face masks would be actually beaten, either by hands or even with rocks or bottles thrown at them. The rebels were treated as devils walking among the saints. Those that experienced this must have felt like those that were killed in Salem during the witch trials."

The media continued to push the recommendations, which were later to become law. Following the Standard Operating Procedures (SOPs such as social distancing and PPE) was not only the right thing to do, but it was cool too, almost superhero worthy.

It also allowed the most powerful a glimpse into who were Sheep, those who would comply with the SOPs whom they could control, and who were Wolves, those who did not comply and refused to follow SOPs.

With 99% of all various media worldwide, the only discussion pushed would be that of COVID-19. The only exception would be President Fowler, but even he was forced to push the COVID-19 Agenda ultimately.

This was the time when individuals and families would begin to choose what side they were on, Sheep or Wolf. For those that didn't decide on their own, the choice would be made by the authorities.

"Sheep are those desired by the elected government officials. After all, the highest-ranking government officials all work for the 1%, and the 1% have all the resources to succeed at what they want most of the time.

"Yes, even the 1% do have defeats and have been on the wrong side throughout history. But even with those previous defeats, the 1% have had record-altering power to change those past defeats into victory.

"All over the United States and worldwide, the vast majority of businesses small and large, corporate or individually owned, did make necessary changes that were being required or implemented for protection.

"These were changes that required spending significant amounts of money to add barriers, create drive-thru service, and purchase cleaning products and PPE for the employees and even clients who may have forgotten or lost their mask.

"The majority of these businesses had to invest in ways to create barriers between the customers and the staff. The government guidelines demand full compliance with the social distancing rule of 6 feet in all directions.

"This social distancing protocol meant that every business would only be allowed to operate at 30-50% of the staff. Even working 24 hours a day, only so much could be done with limited staff. A staff that had been lawfully coerced to be lowered.

"Along the same vein, the businesses were compelled to only allow a limited number of customers in the stores. This was termed as Business Customer Capacity (BCC). This applied to grocery stores, supermarkets, butcher shops, all.

"BCC would also depend on the type of business and the amount of spacing available. This would determine how many could enter and be in legal compliance with the new social distancing requirements.

"Now for the Doctors and Hospitals. When the need for immediate or scheduled medical situations arose, one person at a time would be treated. They, too, would have to be there without any companions or loved ones. Even those near their death due to the virus would not be allowed a final Goodbye.

"This was the result of the effects that were just starting. Yet, the fear was growing like a raging, uncontrollable wildfire.

"The first wave of the COVID-19 saw a scarcity of resources such as water, toilet paper, cleaning products, hand sanitizers. Just about all food sold was instantly out of the markets too. It was the first time in my entire life that this was happening. I would go from store to store, but they were all pretty much empty. Certain necessities were nowhere to be found. This was because of hoarders who were buying everything off the shelves in large quantities.

"However, in a matter of time, things started to return to normal. The shelves began to be replenished. Everything started to show signs of being back to what was normal before COVID-19. Grocery stores such as Walmart, Sam's Clubs, Costco, and Amazon all made record profits.

"Yet for most others, there were losses. This applied especially to the small business owners, which comprised 72% of business owners at this time in history. 28% of the corporations were owned and controlled by the 1%, with the costs of products increasing and wages decreasing for the remaining 99%.

"The big and powerful continued to grow in times of peril, while the others were considered non-essential. They were no longer allowed to operate.

"I am talking about businesses that were no threat to the giant corporations that made Trillions of dollars in profits. Instead, these were the former heartbeat of the US economy.

They were the backbone for a large number of Americans, the former small business owners.

"Small businesses had to adapt. But despite adaptive attempts, things did not work out. Many of them had to cease all operations. Others were ordered and mandated to be entirely closed by Governors of certain States.

"In short, there was not only a national but a global topsy-turvy. Things, as they had always operated, were starting to change. Gaming, Casinos, Bars, Night Clubs, Movie Theaters, Schools, businesses were all shut and ordered to stay home.

"This meant even places like Las Vegas and Nevada that were open 24 hours a day, 7 days a week had to be shut. Individuals worldwide began to stay at home, at least those that were Sheep.

"The only essentials were Hospitals, Police, Fire Department, Grocery Stores like Walmart, pharmacies, and others, similar to the mentioned types of industry. This resulted in an instant 60 million Americans to become unemployed. Until today, we know of this as the worst-ever record in the United States' entire history.

"The world of sports also suffered. Sporting Events, a daily event, such as NBA, NHL, MLB, and even Nascar, had to cancel their seasons mid-way.

"This quarantine was to ensure that the deadly virus that kills 7 people out of every 100,000 people would not spread. With schools closed, we no longer had any High School or even College sports. Even several professional athletes became unemployed.

"With all these measures, people still continued to test positive. The death rates were much lower, though, yet that was never mentioned blatantly. With the increased positive tests, many of which were incorrect, duplicated many times over, as we saw, at least those in the 99% were told that the Coronavirus was still increasing, even though it wasn't.

"The information about the rising cases was the only discussion. This went on both in all forms of media and on the internet. This constant bombardment of fear meant that one thing that vanished was smiles on the partly covered faces. The smiles and facial expressions, which reveal the essence of our humanity, had been replaced with face coverings created by fear.

"There came a time by the end of 2020 when the government was no longer challenged to oppose the SOPs. They knew that the public was both powerless and afraid. The 1% immediately leaped upon the opportunity and created more additional rules. These, too, were lawfully enforced, and were as follows…"

The rules now appeared on the screen.

1) A face mask must be worn at all times; the ONLY exception is while eating or taking a shower.

2) Gloves are to be worn at all times.

3) No shorts, pants only. All tops must be long sleeves at all times.

4) Maintain 6 feet social distance in all directions at all times.

5) Do not touch your face.

6) Wash your hands for 20 seconds with soap after touching anything.

7) Wipe down all you have contacted each and every time contact occurs.

8) Eating is to be done by only one person at a time in Public or Private.

9) Report any illness or symptoms of illness to your Local government Official.

10) Report any of the above when violated to government Enforcement.

The man continued, "A new era was upon all of us worldwide, one that was going to be more dehumanizing than any authoritarian regime. Only 99% were required to follow these new laws.

"The elites, including the elected officials, did not follow any of the rules. Especially not in private settings. Being the rule-maker is above the average Joe. Especially with the new requirements being enforced.

"If you were afraid and terrified, then naturally you didn't mind the requirements and PPE laws. Those who privately disagreed, yet wanted to stay employed, would naturally follow the rules and law when working and in public.

"Most people were unemployed and getting the stimulus benefits regularized by their respective states. The unemployment benefits included a paycheck or debit card, and with the government Stimulus, they would receive an extra $600.00 per week on top of the State pay.

"For a large majority, these combined payments would exceed what they actually made when and while they were working previously. So even if things were to get better, many would rather be paid far greater sums staying home and doing nothing. By working, they were only getting a fraction of what they received while unemployed.

"This seeded the thought in many people. They entertained why work a lot of hours for far less overall actual pay when they were getting more without doing anything? Me personally? Can't say that I blame them. Yet, I was one of those who continued to work each and every day I was scheduled. Quite often, I worked a far greater amount of hours than what my weekly salary paid me.

"Most of the Sheep decided that getting the stimulus was worth all the rules and requirements. That was at least until the governments went broke and could not provide stimulus to those not employed...

"By this time, a new project of testing the vaccines had begun too. Only a handful of people knew that this was happening. It was covert. The person getting the test and the practitioner administering the tests to the different groups did not know they were injecting or being injected with possible experimental vaccines.

"The older testing method for COVID-19 required a sample to be taken from deep inside a nostril. Then came a new method that injected the tester with an experimental vaccine that needed test subjects. In other words, unaware lab rats.

"People were being tested and injected without their consent. As the injected tester would be placed inside a person's nostrils, the tester would also release a potential vaccine for COVID-19.

"This was also the first time in all of recorded or known human history that so many individuals gave up rights to the governments where they lived or resided. These rights, unbeknownst to them, are as precious as your personal DNA samples.

"By agreeing to be tested, which did require consent, we gave the government full permission to use our DNA for current and future projects.

"Think of the phrase 'Do You Really Trust the government?' Well, billions upon billions did. What the government could do with all those DNA test results at present, and also in the future without a single person knowing was beyond our imagination.

"Later, we, of course, did find out what some of those things were. They led to an evolution not even thought of before or considered. Our present now is the product of reactions to the Coronavirus-19 Requirements and Laws for all of mankind.

"Every human is born with natural defenses that fight germs and viruses. So, when a person is getting a flu shot, that shot comprises of the same flu virus, the person has been injected in low doses. Why? To jump-start the natural defenses to fight the virus and build up a person's resistance towards that virus.

"Then you have the humans that are entirely immune to COVID-19 – the immune-resistant one, if I may scientifically call them. It would have been those that could have possibly aided in creating an effective vaccine. But alas…

"Before I explain what happened to most of them, allow me to explain something about the virus. DNA is the map that contains your genetic information. It can tell experts things that make you valuable in ways a normal thinking person would never consider valuable. You can turn out to be the savior or doom-bringer for millions, just based on your DNA sample.

"With billions of people worldwide submitting their DNA via testing, the greatest collection of human DNA happened. In the right hands, this meant a possible cure or vaccine. In the wrong hands, a new method of controlling the masses and population.

"Against the Immuno-resistant masses, there were many more of those who were vulnerable to the virus. Those that most-needed the cure. When the time came, the immune-resistant individuals disappeared, never seen or heard from ever again since 2021.

"Those who are immune are, for the most part, those who are known as the Wolves, for the majority of them did not subject themselves or those they love to the testing…"

Matthew now waved to the woman with the tattoo, who paused the video on the screen. "I have a question," he asked meekly.

The woman came near to him and asked him intently, "What's the problem?"

"Don't get me wrong, all this info is... enlightening to me... But can we take a break for a little while? I really gotta go to the bathroom now..."

The woman straightened up with a poker face, broke into a frown, and gestured Matthew to follow her.

Chapter 3
The Sheep

Matthew flushed the toilet and walked out of the grungy bathroom. The woman waited outside for him with arms crossed. The man with dreads was with her now.

"Okay, are we ready to continue the film?" Matthew asked.

"Documentary," the woman's piercing voice said, "It's not a movie, not a fiction, it's a documentary. This is actually happening out there."

"Yes, yes, of course. I didn't mean it like tha-"

"Just sit down and watch the damn thing," the man with the dreads spoke now.

Matthew did as was asked.

The man in the lab coat paused on the screen continued now.

"Opposed to the Wolves are Sheep, as I've briefly mentioned before. These people believe everything that is on the News, Media, Television, Magazines, Music, and the

Internet. If Margot Robbie says her next movie is a must-watch, they believe it. If Shawn Mendes announces he doesn't think environmental change is real, they believe him. The government tells them Coronavirus is fatal, they believe it.

"They accept all sources of knowledge that keep them 'safe,' keeping their own restricted idea of safety in mind. The vast majority of the Sheep will follow whatever rules, regulations, instructions, ideologies are thrust upon them without much question. The Media and government are their only Gods.

"The Sheep also believe that government is for the people and will protect the weak. They consider themselves weak and those that need help. The Wolves scoff at this idea. The Sheep truly believe in this and lean on the government to take care of them and protect them. 'We pay taxes, after all,' they say. 'The government will not cause us any trouble,' they also say.

Sheep are also the ones that have been the most fearful of COVID-19, that deadly virus that kills 7 people out of 100,000. After all, factually speaking, every single day before the year 2020 and before the COVID-19, 156,000 people died on average. Not in one country, not in a single continent, but all around the world."

"Yes, this *is* a large number. 156,000 people on average, before COVID-19, died daily. Due to non-COVID illnesses, needless to say. This is not 7 people out of 100,000 over 7 months. This is not 580,000 people from December 2019 to July 2020. The Sheep failed to realize how small this number amounted to.

"Another event that was not brought before the public eye was that for the first time in nearly 100 years, the rate of birth had significantly decreased all over the world. Fewer newborns coming into the world meant that the birth to death ratio was reducing. It first came to notice in 2021.

"This was how things were to continue for the next few years. Every year fewer newborns were being born. The people in the large metropolitan cities were no longer enjoying life as they once did. The standards of living decreased for the rich and poor, the urban and rural alike. The number of people having sex also decreased. Many thought that having sex would give them the Coronavirus. Needless to say again, the ones who believed that were the Sheep.

"Marriage rates also dropped by over 85% during 2021. The PPE businesses were generating truckloads of money because of the fear that made the Sheep spend on masks, gloves, antibacterial soap, disinfectants. The economy continued to spiral even lower for the other 99% worldwide.

"This was true for what was happening to those that lived in the Major Cities. The population stagnated, fewer marriages took place, and certainly, very little to no sexual relations existed between men and women. Life had indeed changed, especially for those in metropolitan cities.

"Yet for those who rebelled and predominantly lived in the Country, the Wolves, things weren't so bad. They continued to have marriages, relationships, and far greater birth rates than those of the larger cities and places with enormous populations.

"Nearly 120 million Americans had now become unemployed, and another 50 Million or so were under-employed. Inflation reached an all-time high. All prices kept rising, be it food or medicine. Some people had to choose between the two, especially with the added costs of having Personal Protection Equipment.

"The 1% elites of the world with all of these changes shifted their industrial processes to Robotics. With unemployment already on the rise, the remaining workers also got replaced by machines. The automated production and substitution of people that started with the superpower countries first became possible worldwide. All the jobs that needed a human driver became extinct.

"The economy worldwide started declining by the hour. Even though life had taken a downward turn for the Wolves and others that lived in the smaller communities, they could survive it. They were not nearly as affected as those that lived in the larger cities.

"The poor became poorer, the 1% and a few others made more money than ever before compared to pre-Corona times. The Sheep stayed home, doing as they were instructed. They never asked what the COVID-19 death rates were based on. They never questioned anything.

"Had the Sheep done that and inquired about the death rates or advancement of robots and machines taking away jobs, things would not have been the way they are today. The Sheep more than likely also would have rebelled if they stopped eating what they were fed.

"By 2022, the COVID-19 had basically infected all people, and we, the vast majority, did survive. Especially since the death rate was now at 7 people per million due to COVID-19. Only the scientists that were Wolves investigated this phenomenon. Yet that was never discussed nor told by the Media. All they chased, backed up by the 1%, was the goal of complete control. They believed that it was closer than ever before.

"For those that continued to stay in major cities, the new normal of life continued. It dictated: always wear a face mask, always have on gloves, do not touch anything: wash your hands, do not touch your face, keep a social distance of 6 feet or further in all directions at all times, eat alone and in private and do not have sex or exchange any type of body fluids.

"There were no more jobs. Everybody started relying on the government for food; shelter was for the strongest, for, after all, even the police were no more. People were without any guns to protect themselves in the larger cities. Due to that, the death rates became far greater than COVID-19. COVID-19 could have continued for a hundred years and still not achieve that death rate.

"Eventually, the government decided to place further restrictions. For anyone to have sex with another person, now required approval. This approval would require that a person has the means to fulfill the testing and paperwork necessary. For those in the 99%, that could not happen for most had little to no money for the testing alone.

"How was this new law surveilled? The same way all other laws were being surveilled now by the robots.

"Soon things became such that every death was a consequence of COVID-related restrictions or sanctions, instead of the actual disease. These were all the real, actual crimes perpetrated by the 1% of the world. But all urge or impulse for protesting had been killed with the government and media's ideological state apparatus, as Louis Althusser called it. No one rose up against the violence of the rich. They were the only ones who enjoyed the new normal... which was only going to get worse."

Hearing all this, and being shown all the graphs and tables, Matthew had been sitting shocked and unblinking all this while. But it was the last sentence that had made him say his first word after long minutes: "Oh, damn."

Chapter 4
The Wolves

The man with the dreads and the woman in the tank top paused the screen and looked at Matthew.

"Good timing," said the woman. "That's the end of this part. Do you have any questions so far?"

"I do have some. The more challenging ones I won't answer already because I'm trying to figure them out on my own."

The man and the woman looked at one another.

"I mean, I wouldn't be alarmed if I was you, nahhh," he waved his wrist at the two.

The woman tapped her foot. The lack of ventilation was evident in the room. All three were sweating inside their clothes thoroughly, but neither of them complained. Sweat had begun the most natural part about being alive, given the new world order.

"First question, when are you guys going to scavenge next?"

"That is your concern how?" The man with folded arms and dreads squinted at Matthew.

Matthew rolled his eyes and casually looked around the room. On one corner of the room, a sleek, broken vase stood. Entangled to it were some dark green vines – at least that was the color Matthew could tell from the bleak lighting – that seemed to be growing out of nowhere. They looked like beach reeds to him. Matthew was surprised by how he could remember that childhood memory after all those years. The boy thought it was a weird shelf as he turned his gaze away from it and looked at his guards.

"Well, food, of course! You guys don't have anything to eat in here, and I deserve some snacks if you are going to continue the mov- I mean, documentary. I'm dead-ass serious right now."

The man with the dreads was ready to pull his gun out, but the woman extended her hand and kept him from sounding any gunfire. They couldn't kill the kid, at least not without any proper reason. Matthew looked calm on the surface, but he felt like he would pee in his pants.

"There's an old tin can of soup we had found hidden in rubble." The woman pulled it out from her back pocket and threw it towards Matthew. He caught it effortlessly, then looked up in anticipation.

"Well," he said.

"Well what," came the reply.

"Where is the can opener?"

The man cowered at Matthew and then, knitting his eyebrows, whispered something in the woman's ear. The only word Matthew could catch was "confusing." He then went forth and punched a hole in the tin using his bare teeth. Matthew had the canned soup in his hands now.

"OK, I'm ready to watch this now!"

The old man in the lab coat seamlessly continued, "Now, we talk about the Wolves. Wolves are those individuals that typically live in the country or in small towns throughout America. These people usually live in places where the rules of requiring a mask, wearing gloves, wearing only pants, and long sleeve clothing are not enforced. You heard it right, the government-enforced rules were not followed in the territory of the Wolves. They didn't believe in the requirements of social distancing either.

"Since Wolves, for the most part, did not follow nor believe in social distancing, their faith in government Testing was extremely low too. And by that, I mean they did not get themselves tested. For the Wolves, the lifestyle typically would be to meet, socialize, drink, smoke, party, have sex, frolic around and do the things which were once normal. They were the 'You Only Live Once' kind, if I say so myself. In the past, and even in today's world, these activities are considered illegal, with the residual authority left in the government's hand.

"The majority of adult and teenage Wolves typically do work, and they work hard. One strand of Wolves does follow the directions and ethics of employment, which would require Sheep-like compliance only in order to keep a job. They knew their hypocrisy, though. These Wolves were not like the country Wolves; instead, they were the city Wolves.

"If you ask me, I think the better-coined name for the City Wolves was 'Wolf in Sheep's clothing.' This held its weight since a large amount of the Wolves did indeed also live and reside in large cities. They put up an exterior to a certain point to blend in with the crowds, but in private, the real city Wolves did not follow the rules. They would socialize and gather with other like-minded city Wolves quite often. City Wolves had a much harder time and many more obstacles than the country Wolves…"

"Wait, can you pause for a second," Matthew said.

"I swear if you say something goofy…"

"No, I only mean to ask that the Wolves, they would carry out their parties in private, of course, right?"

The man and the woman looked at each other and told him, "Yes." They were surprised Matthew was taking an interest. He nodded his head and continued slurping the soup.

"For a country Wolf or those who are from a small town with limited technology, the law is not something made to be feared. The law is enforced by and through the locals of each town, city, and state, and the country Wolves lived beyond that jurisdiction.

"Even with the State in charge of State matters, each State doesn't have the resources to enforce every single town and country, especially those that do live in remote areas such as farmers, ranchers, small towns, small cities or out remotely in the country."

"The new rules were not possible to be enforced if the Wolves got away with breaking the new rules of society without getting caught. In their small territories, the enforcement of the law was not being pushed by the locals. This scenario is applied worldwide.

"Country Wolves also had the ability to control exactly what their children learned. After the change brought about by 2020 some of the events that transpired historically started getting removed from the history books. A new history was being invented to make the masses happy.

"Rather than keeping the past as it was, numerous changes were being made. History was literally being re-written, and new movements were being created to replace the ones that had actually occurred.

"Statues were being removed, team names, professional and college sports team names were being changed, mainly for being considered as racists. This depended on the ethnicity and nationality of people too.

"One important reason why that traumatized life on earth as we knew it was because we comprehend our present by studying our history. Mistakes that happened in the past are patterned. They have tell-tale signs and lessons which we are not to repeat. Those that have learned the actual history of the past diligently know about the pattern of events that may repeat again.

"To have that knowledge and to learn from it is empowering. That's what has created revolutionary leaders in the past. But the new-world order decimated that possibility. The end result was a society with far fewer Wolves than Sheep. History gave us hope in the past, but around the history-altering period of humanity, we were riding into a darker tunnel.

"The tradition of history, however, continued for All the Wolves, country, city or wherever they resided. Wolves were teaching their children to include events of the past History, the good and the bad, and learn from it. Since the schools had all been shut down, all education was and is self-taught. Only those who have money can afford the internet, which is necessary to access schooling and bring it to the young minds of the world. This possibility was open only to those who were in the City.

"Country Wolves may or may not have the internet, yet they have always been capable of living life regardless. They believe that certain liberties are for all life, not just those in the 1% or the high-ranking government officials. This is also true for the City Wolves, or at least the majority of them.

"City Wolves, however, do require the internet for they rely on technology. Again, the country Wolves are OK with or without technology; some spend all their lives without holding cell phones or using the internet. Social Media may just be a myth to them.

"City Wolves have greater responsibility on their shoulders. They must be able to blend in and appear to be a Sheep without ever giving it away. However, city Wolves do have the privilege of what is called sit-ins. Sit-ins are where other like-minded "City Wolves" gather at a person's location or a place and discuss their plans and troubles.

"After their discussions, the city Wolves then will go as rowdy as the country Wolves: they would drink, smoke cigarettes or marijuana, and have sex. It would all happen without face masks. These parties would, of course, be highly illegal, especially in the larger cities. The Wolves, though, knew a thing or two about how not to get caught. This included knowing where the populations are great.

"They have to be careful for it is common to be turned in by a Sheep. The price to pay for violations of this nature would normally mean utter disappearance. The apprehended Wolves are never seen or heard from again.

"Wolves are also the people that have not subjected themselves to providing the government the right to test for COVID. They are also subjected to being injected with some trial-unapproved vaccine for testing.

"As for the Country Wolves, they would not have to worry about testing centers because their population does not meet the required level of residents and are bypassed, excluding all the residents of remote locations and smaller communities.

"Since all ages were then required for testing by the government in the normal and larger cities, more than enough crews of authorities were trained and authorized to do as they wished and desired. There would be no security forces in the country, though.

"Life for the Country Wolves compared to the City Wolves has a greater history, for the country areas were where the Wolves first arose. They have lived and occupied the same territory for a greater amount of time.

"Many small towns and communities have residents that may date back to several generations or older. In these communities, it is typical for everyone to know everyone. This applies to the United States as it does for places worldwide where little to no technology now remains.

"For a City Wolf, that has never really been the case. The vast majority of a city's population has a history fraught with the migration of every few years. The world had not seen such division nor arrangement of people before the COVID virus breakout.

"City Wolves have always existed as a much more careful and vulnerable part of society. They have had to be far more selected of whom they interact with. This goes for especially their work colleagues or neighbors they have ties with.

"That may not be the case after all for those that are true sheep. Their fears have not comprised of this variant of fear. They are on the lookout for Wolves and would indeed turn in any Wolf to the authorities without any remorse or second thoughts. These sanctions make life much tougher and harder for the city Wolves than the country Wolves.

"And then, of course, cities are far greater in technology. Cameras are everywhere; people are constantly being watched and recorded on their phones, tablets, etc. These are devices that everyone other person carries. One never knew who may be watching them, so a city Wolf always had to be on their guard.

"At the end of the day, the Wolves are all Wolves. Those of the Wolf clan that had been open rebels have demanded their rights even in the city. Wolves have also educated themselves of how things were before them being a Wolf. They have preserved all knowledge and oppose the brainwashing fed by the government. This includes things that the Sheep consider beneficial to themselves, such as mandatory welfare.

"To the Wolves, Covid and the government go hand in hand. The latter wanted a full-blown takeover, like an authoritarian regime. They wanted to kill all signs of rebellion, which meant snatching the guns from people so that they cannot stand up against the powerful. Also important to mention is the fact that most of the Police Departments have been defunded. The concept of police has been made a thing of the past.

"The Wolves are from all political walks of life, 'Democrats, Republicans, and Independents alike. Wolves have never endorsed conventional ethics among them. Wolves are typically resilient and resistant to believing mass media-propagated information that they read or hear.

"Wolves certainly do not like Big government. They hate being told how to live life. To nearly half the world, these people are considered outright outlaws; to the other half, they are Heroes.

"The 1% of people worldwide are made up of individuals and families that come from a wide variety of locations all over the World. Because of the wealth, they have amassed, they also have all the power in their territories.

"The vast majority of the 1% have, for the most part, been born into their luxurious lifestyle. The majority of them have been generationally elite. They have been agenda-pushers of their ancestry for centuries now. For some of them, their fate was sealed to be what they are before they were even born. They are raised with one goal in mind: Total Control of Everything and Everyone.

"The 1% of the world chase that phenomenon. They desire to be the only Rich and Powerful people to exist. They have no fear for the governments, nor for elected officials. They believe the government can easily be replaced, and its members soon forgotten.

"Oblivion goes for Presidents just as it does for sitting members of either the House of Congress or those that are State Senators. These latter two positions do not have term limits. It is an amazing position of puppeteering. It makes an average Sheep get elected to one of these Cabinets, only to leave as a multi-millionaire with a degree of power, if they do well. That also ensures for them a lifetime of benefits that every American would love to have.

"Yet to the 1%, those in politics would only be what a manager or employee would be to a business owner. In this case, the business owners are the 1%. The politicians, they do matter, yet they do not matter. The highest-ranking officials are and have been controlled by the 1% for a long time.

"Since the government Officials are very greedy, corrupt, and self-centered, they only care to achieve more power and gain greater wealth. As I have said, these government members involved in this are the true exemplars of Sheep.

"Here's the twisted aspect, they may personally believe and think that they are Wolves, but they are not. That alone makes the 1% comfortable. However, the actual Wolves existing in the world are the one and only thing that makes the 1% uncomfortable.

"The 1% truly believes that the Wolves, no matter where they are on the globe, are terrorists. They are the only threat to their generational mission of Total Control Worldwide.

"The Wolves in the near future seek to be the group that fights for all mankind. They wish to convert and lead the Sheep too. They know of themselves as the only chance to save all of mankind. They know that the hope for survival rests on their shoulders the most heavily."

Matthew stood up from his seat without any warning. "I cannot take this anymore. I have wanted to sit here and watch silently but goddamn. They really have hidden so much from us?"

Matthew looked desperately and the nonchalant faces of his guards. "They did us all pretty bad, I'll tell ya."

The woman asked him this time, "Do you have any more questions from us so far?"

"Alright fine, I'll finally ask it of you. You guys brought me here because I'm a potential Wolf, I mean, that's the reason you brought me here right?"

The two people standing gave each other a tight-lipped smile before turning to Matthew again.

Chapter 5
The Guns

Outside the shutters where the projector played, a small society resided. The sun shone on the dull grass. A din of kids sounded on the side. They stood frolicking, unpoetic, and unruly—hair long and wild, bodies bare as if they were raised by Tarzan. The children cackled and laughed. They splashed water on each other's lean and developing bodies, on which sweat and the swamp had merged indubitably. Nearby, women washed clothes, and around the banks of the huge pond laid belts upon belts equipped with firearms.

***

"We cannot answer that just yet," said the man with dreadlocks. He picked up a rugged toothpick from near his boots and put that to his mouth. "You would have to complete watching the whole thing first."

"No surprise; none at all for me. I was gonna ask that question later anyway." Matthew shrugged. "Press play on the damn thing already. Ma would be waiting for me."

"Don't be worried about, Ma," said the woman as she got the documentary rolling.

"How much time until this ends, by the way," Matthew asked over the scientist speaking as he gestured towards the screen.

The woman gave him a deadly stare that said enough to Matthew. He turned around to the projector screen.

"With the police force getting fully defunded, the next thing that the 1% wanted and really desired was that all of those who belong to the 99% were disallowed guns. That's why they changed gun rights in the legislation. Guns were made completely illegal for any civilian to hold.

"When this got announced, even some of the Sheep stood up and complained. That was fresh for the Wolves to see. But the 1% did not budge. For them, this was the perfect opportunity to now snatch away all the guns from every single American, nationwide, and worldwide.

"All the Police departments were disbanded, defunded, and closed down nationally as per the New President's executive orders. The system of law and order was no longer followed in America. The 1% and the "managers" who worked for the 1%, the highest-ranking members of the government, ensured the closure of all Police Departments on a personal level. Not a single one was to remain.

"A large percentage of the Sheep was joyous that the Police Departments shut down. After all, many of the Sheep had been wanting that to happen for years. They felt the Police were a nuisance and their corruption made them appear Wolf-like. The Sheep celebrated their disbandment with the 1%.

"Yet, the same Sheep that were glad to see the Police defunded later came to regret that. They later wished for the Police to be allowed, even tried to start a movement. But by that time, it was too late.

"Among those that identified as Sheep, many still had very mixed feelings about making all guns completely illegal and outlawed. Even the Sheep needed protection, some instrument of self-defense, right? Some of those Sheep, rather than complaining and protesting, began to leave the cities and decided to join the Wolves.

"It was officially announced that all weapons, including guns, rifles, assault weapons, and anything that fired a bullet, were illegal and had to be turned over to the government immediately. No one was to have any type of gun. If caught, they would be taken away to never be seen or heard from again.

"This hit the gun collectors pretty badly, especially those with antique weaponry. The 1% enjoyed that torture. Except for these very people and those that served and protected them, such as bodyguards and security detail, none of the official civilians possessed any weapons, at least not among the Sheep.

"The high-ranking government officials were also the only groups that would, from this point forward, be legally allowed to own, operate or have in their possession firearms, along with those who protected them.

"For anyone else to be able to have any gun protection required that they hire a government-approved and appointed, legally-licensed bodyguard. Again, this would require the people seeking this permit and approval to be affluent members of society. The only truly affluent ones were the 1%. That meant all the "Others," the remaining 99%, had no legal way of owning guns.

"Most of the Sheep had fully agreed with the government and thought that a world without guns would be a safer and happy place for all citizens. They were too blinded to see that the place they lived in was filled with chaos and anarchy. The one exception and some semblance of lawfulness remained in wearing of the masks and following the other Covid-related rules.

"With time, things proved to be the exact opposite. Without guns, a person in a lawless society was ruled over by the ruthless who had the strongest physicality. Those that lived in smaller communities, the Wolves, had not turned over their guns. Instead, they started to prepare their own bullets and began to stockpile guns and ammunition, for they knew they would need them one day. In a system of anarchy, the probability of war breaking out was not a small one.

"With the new Gun Act put in place, the next industry to shut down and become 100% illegal was bullet manufacturers. The rationale given for this was, "Sure, some people will still rebel, they'll keep their guns. But without bullets, how dangerous can a gun really be?"

"Without the Police or weapons to protect civilians, anarchy and chaos rose at an all-time high. The new world order for the 99% had already begun. It was based on strength, which they ruled over by using Fear.

"After all, think about it, without police or guns who was going to be available to stop the crimes and evil that was growing by the hour?"

"Life in the cities was now filled with the Sheep. The people who belonged to the Wolves side had now started to leave those large cities. They were not about to give up the guns which protected them.

"The Sheep that were physically the strongest, especially those in the larger cities, by early 2024 had begun ruling different parts of the cities they belonged to. They brought no new ideas for the betterment of the people, yet were elected easily. The 1% found their world domination tactic safe with them, and so they allowed their regimes.

"The only thing that the enforcement would intervene was if it involved a gun or if people were not wearing a mask. It has been as silly a deal as it sounds, trust me. Even the hobos living on the streets or homeless people hiding near the bridges wore masks.

"The guns had already been confiscated in all the major cities of the world. Having a gun and being caught with it meant instant death in many of the countries.

"Guns became a very rare commodity. They were hard to find illegally in black markets as well as with people, because most of the Sheep had returned the guns, including some City Wolves. The idea of protection no longer existed as it was before the Age of Gunlessness. Violent physical force was used without any worries of being prosecuted or getting into any trouble by people. A fascinating evolutionary regression this was.

"The 1% did not care about that. They let the other 99% rot in their savagery.

"Too many glass ceilings were put in the system. To reach the 1% became almost as high as owning a gun. Accessing highly illegal weapons would require deep pockets. And then acquiring bullets was another matter. To have a gun and no bullets was useless. Thus, a loaded gun was as difficult a commodity to obtain as finding someone belonging to the 1% on the anarchic streets. Bullets were another expense that only those with the greatest wealth could afford.

"All of the drastic changes were brought with the onset of the current President, who by the way has been rumored to have died a while ago. The President who was not even seen nor heard in public for almost 3 years."

Matthew raised his hand. "How old even is this documentary. This guy knows everything. Does he know I'm sitting here and watching him right now?"

The man and the woman gave Matthew intense stares before playing the documentary again.

"The Sheep that did comply and remained behind in the city became exactly what the 1% desired. The 'masses that did not matter.' They were unable to revolt, and all the fight had been defeated in them.

"Yet, for those that knew the Wolves were not a myth, they did fear them. The Wolves were the only group who had their weapons and were well-stocked. To acquire bullets for the Wolves was no difficulty. They had become skilled in making their own bullets in no time. They were also capable of reproducing those bullets when needed or required. And yes, I will say this again; they were stockpiling both guns and ammo.

"For the Wolves to comply by giving the government the guns, which the majority of Wolves owned, was a disgrace. Death was a better option. The government would have to remove the guns from their dead bodies. The Wolves were dead-serious about fighting for the right to bear arms to their death.

"This status quo that had begun years ago continues to remain the same to date. These are all norms today.

"The Sheep did agree with the results of every election that has taken place since 2020. Their favorite candidates were Elected, the Police were defunded and shut down. Gun Control was now illegal. Masks were required, and laws were created to ensure that the SOPs and PPE were still in place. All of these things gave the Sheep a semblance of safety. They trusted the government.

"The crime and chaos were worse than any other time in all of history. But their trust in the government remained because the media never talked about 'negative' things.

"For those who identify as Wolves, they knew that it was for the first time ever in America's voting history that all the ballots were mailed in. There were no more voting stations, rather elections happened 100% mail-in only. Yes, a fix was in, after all, nearly 27.4 million votes were later found to be from non-citizen's or those who were deceased when the 2020 Election took place. Don't even ask me about 2024, though. Even the Wolves learned about the 2020 Election fiasco several years later, when the greater changes happened."

Matthew waved for a pause and scratched his head. "Before we get to any bigger changes, let me first say this. I knew about most of the things the documentary is talking about now, but I did not know how it originated from. In that way, it's all coming together for me."

"That was the plan," came the reply.

"Secondly," Matthew says as he scratches his chin, "I think the soup went down to my bladder. I need to pee again."

"Honestly," the man with the dreads said to the woman, "I am not even surprised by this guy anymore." And then he led Matthew to the washroom again.

Some distance away, the howling sounds of the Wolves could be heard.

Chapter 6
The Beginnings

There were many things different in the world of 2026, but all around, some things were common. One would look at it and perceive that the sky was brown, but it was only the filter of dust. The air was stale and stolid. The city was molding like being consumed by gangrene. Smokes from whatever remaining vehicles that ran were the figment of algae. Roads had forgotten any spectacle of civility.

By 2026, metropolitan life as the world knew of before had completely changed. The cities were filled with Sheep, where the state of anarchy had riddled holes in humanity's idea that had proceeded since John Locke's 'Tabula Rasa' concept. From a distance, the cities looked like a sewer, and morality-wise, it felt the same. All of them alike.

Amidst the sea of vehicles, not the sharpest eye could look and find a police vehicle. Not the most diligent looker could sift past the rotting buildings and pick out a law enforcement building or station because there was none to find anymore. But something that even the blind person didn't need eyes to see the gruesome crimes of violence.

Governance, the commodity that rested in the pocket of the strongest, had become mega corrupt. The 5% of the governing body was always around, even in their invisibility. Like Big Brother, they were always watching. They were the unseen puppeteers in the air tossing apples of discord and enabling theft, rape, murder.

What the eye of the Big Brother most religiously followed were faces. At this point, sometimes even without endorsing it, everybody followed the COVID-19 SOPs. There always had to be a mask on every face at all visible times. Whether one had a mouth or not, on their face had to be, and usually used to be, the required face mask. On the hands, there were gloves worn at all times.

Supermarkets with broken windows and damaged goods looked scared every morning that people awoke. It would just be another day of riot for transactions. They knew it. The more resourceful stores had gotten baseball bats wrapped in barbed wire for their employees to prevent disorder. Every employee was additional security, along with the guards who also held the same weaponry. None could afford the guns; the smaller stores could not even afford brawling weapons.

And even as citizens raided the stores and ensured they robbed them clean, they wore masks and gloves. Any citizen found with their masks and gloves off for as long as three hours was met with kidnapped disappearance. Out of thin air, the COVID-26

Enforcement would ram in, and everybody would freeze with awe and terror. A team of people wearing hazmat suits would climb out of their vans, with futuristic-looking guns in their hands, carrying the criminal violator, and poof. The 'rebel' would never be seen or heard from again. The families all knew that hoping was hopeless.

Among people that wore masks at all times, the largest percentage was that of Sheep. All of the Sheep lived in much larger cities with Wolf in Sheep's clothing too. They followed all directions and never questioned. Instead, they complied and endorsed the government-supported ideas. These people regularly conducted tests for COVID-19, generally every three months, to make sure they were sage. They always wore their masks, 24 hours a day, seven days a week. By this time, water-resistant masks with slits for eating food had already been introduced to facilitate the agenda better.

In the hospitals, COVID-19 was the disease predominantly being tested for. This polarization meant two things. Someone who had other conditions would fail to learn about it. And secondly, a novel and different type of virus could infect and spread, and the medical health specialists would not even be aware of it. Years and years of human beings losing their civility and wearing masks for protection yielded in a rupture. They were not allowing their genes that lie inherently to tackle the virus any longer. The human body got subjected to its lack of use of antibodies. They severely weakened. It had now become easier for any virus to attack and grow.

And that was just what happened with the creation of COVID-26.

***

Amidst one of the supermarket riots, a man who typically participated vehemently in the violence felt particularly feverish one morning. Grabbing his head with one hand and stomach with another, he waited for something – vomit, spit, blood – to come out of him. The nausea was asphyxiating. He sweated till droplets leaked off from him, and his vision blurred and distorted as obnoxious shapes entered and metamorphosed.

"Jesus, I can't- breathe," he wheezed and cough. He did not know that the accumulation of the last six years of his Sheepish human activities had built up into what he was now experiencing. His spinal cord had long been affected by a virus that was climbing upward towards his brain. It was a virus that started off like rabies but was much more deadly.

The man was soon to experience a transformation into a creature that was going to be called 'Z.' He was to be the first of its kind. The damage, however, had already been done. More victims were to now follow at an exponential rate.

The Sheep and City Wolves alike had been wearing the masks that may have been innovated technology-wise, but not many had been ensuring they came with filters. The enforced focus detailed wearing the masks without any other prescription. With the all-time high inflation and inaccessibility of resources, most of those living in the major cities were only buying food from the money they had. They could barely leave room for soap or acquire clean water. They were washing the dishes with filthy water. Disinfecting masks had become a rare practice.

A new breed of bacteria had begun circulating in the city. It found its perfect culmination by combining with the filthy unfiltered masks. The germs created a new strain of COVID that was being termed as Vid-26 or 26-Z Virus; it was the perfect name. After all, the 26th letter of the alphabet is Z.

No one had ever thought, not even the 5%, that the masks themselves would create a Super Flu, which would end up becoming the Zombie reaction. What was manifesting in 2026 had begun in 2020 when masks became mandatory. The testing centers had secretly begun testing insane amounts of vaccines too. These were being given to large groups without their knowledge when they came for the COVID-19 test.

Certain groups of Sheep had been tested with different vaccines. All of them had shown different results. Their immune systems changed according to the wide variety of 'antidotes,' which the experimental vaccines being injected into the Sheep were fancily being called for the past six years.

Once the virus discovery broke, even the media freaked out more than before. The myth of the zombies had been a long time coming, after all. Reporters ran after doctors to discover what the different experimental vaccines contained. The only notes discovered by one of the few doctors who had 'mysteriously' committed suicide showed one of the 35 groups within the range of A-1 to A-35.

All the people had names starting with 'A,' and the last name on the list was Adrian. While the group numbers were discovered, two major questions remained unanswered. How many different groups were there after all, and what was in each of the different vaccines transmitted to each of the groups.

Who knows, perhaps they had thousands of different vaccines to experiment with? For all that the scientists could estimate, there were at least 1000 different groups, given 1000 different vaccines.

The Z Virus turned out to be a prequel to the Zombie virus. The Z's and the Zombies were not the same after all. The Zombies could resuscitate from their death; The Z virus did not revive the dead. Instead, it struck the Sheep living in the large cities who had been wearing a face mask at all times. They self-created the Z virus by following the Rules.

Among the Sheep that turned into Z's, some of them eventually transformed into Zombies. Unlike the Z's who changed because of the combination of the mask and bacteria, the Zombies were born out of the Z's who had been subjected to vaccine testing in the past. In other words, Zombies also wore masks at all times and were injected during one of the tests with a possible vaccine.

This was another failure of humankind. The germs were created out of a combination of vaccine injections that should have been a cure. But that backfired to create the deadliest creature that man could ever turn into; a Zombie.

More instances around the US started popping up of Z's and Zombies after the first case outside the supermarket.

In Albuquerque, news reports showed that those who kept the combination of the Mask and one of the vaccines, after transforming into Z, became unable to walk or move at all. They kept losing one bodily function after another until they died a prolonged and horrible death. They would soon enough rise from their grave, but never as the person they were a few ago.

In New York City too, millions instantly died as the transformations began. They, also, were those that maintained wearing masks and were injected a testing vaccine. Many of those that died started to dry out and lost all body fluids. By the end, the tedious and excruciating deaths were too much for the family to bear.

When the transformations began in Chicago, many Zs with the mask and vaccine combination began to feel their heads shrinking. This was followed by their eyes popping out as their head grew smaller than that of a new born's. Eventually, even their head popped like a giant pimple, splattering brains despite all the doctors' attempts.

In Los Angeles, millions upon millions began to, in the literal sense, burn up. It started with a fever. The next thing they knew, a fire was coming out of an infected mouth and nose. The eyes blacked to the color of coal and burned out. People were melting all around into a pile of sticky goo.

The only ones surviving around these cities were certain City Wolves and those rare Sheep that were immune to the virus because of their natural defense. Yet, these human survivors were in the minority. Z and Zombies were far greater and were taking over by the hour.

Chapter 7
The Zombies

Allie leaned against a car, or barely so. His hand went to the bonnet but slipped. Muscle strength was wavering, he noticed. His hands seemed as damp as of someone who had just submerged them into water. It was his sweat.

The ache in the head was eating him away. With some remaining strength, he was forced to pull his mask down to breathe. When he breathed, he felt as if a fire or smoke expelled.

Inside his body, anarchy had ensued. Magma, in his veins, was eating away all muscle memory. Down came his knee, flat against the asphalt. With vertigo before his eyes, he was near to falling when something changed in his eyes.

"Are you okay?" someone asked him from over his shoulders as he tried to slip out his wallet. Allie grabbed his arm with a force that seared his fingerprints on it. The gloves on the Z's hand burned away. The man cried, but his cry was only going to rise louder.

In one swift motion, Allie brought his mouth down and gnashed. Away pulled his mouth, and a chunk of meaty, bloody flesh tore into his mouth, which he chewed raw, at an uncannily tranquil pace. The man next to him was fainting with pain. As soon as he saw a dog to his left bark, he was about to consume it too, but COVID Enforcement had already arrived.

They tased the creature, astounded inside their yellow hazmat suits and respirators. They were to find out soon this was the first Z out of tremendously more to come.

***

The experimentations on the new creatures had already begun. The 1%_were interested and generously funded research.

A pattern was developing in the habits of Z's. Scientists started noticing that when a Z encountered a defenseless Human who was very ill during the first three weeks, the Z would acknowledge that person but would refrain from bothering that ill human. Apart from that person, they would eat anything with flesh - Older people, babies, all human beings, cats, rats, raw fish with scales, and bones.

Soon enough, this idea developed, and a new discovery was made; that too, beyond the lab. A Z was refraining from eating ill humans for a reason. It figured that the human was yet to transform from Human to Z to Zombie. Thus, they left them alone.

How did they know it? Was it a scent, instinct, or something more? This link between the Z and Zombies. It did not matter for them that a defenseless ill human was the easiest to feed on. It was as if the concept of sacrifice existed among them.

The human, which was transforming into a Zombie, was too weak to move. Not all underwent a transformation as swiftly as Allie. Some would remain ill for days before mutating. They couldn't defend themselves.

It was about three weeks after the first Z was spotted that the first Zombie appearance came about. Within 21 days, the Earth officially had two new species. Their names were acknowledged, and all the data available was disseminated.

Within the first two months, most controllable Sheep included 20% Humans and 80% Z or Zombies. This was the data in major Cities where surveys were possible.

***

The small cities, towns in remote locations, farmers, ranchers, those that love living in the country were all places where such data could not be gathered. What was the scenario there? Mask enforcement wasn't followed there. In these locations, the required testing was not a necessity. Negligence served them well, for no unknown injections were being administered.

These areas and parts of not just America but also the rest of the world had zero to little related transformations of Z or Zombies. Wolves were purely Wolves still, living a mellow life.

They splashed and sang and danced and hunted for wild animals. Loincloths were just as uncriticized among them as pants and jackets. No one was under the obligation to follow what they did not want to follow. Primitive was their existence; a combination of Stoic and Epicurean was their lives.

***

News reports in the metropolitans released extensive information about the new pandemic. It had spread worldwide, and so the precautions were at just as virulent pace. The Z and Zombies had characteristics that made them similar, yet certain unique ones made them very different.

Doctors on every news channel had begun explaining the same thing in different words using various resources. They explained that Z largely remained of the same height as the host with the same face. The distinctive features were eyes that turned pitch black. They had small yet sharp teeth, like dogs. These creatures did not rest nor sleep.

Certain footages went up on the screen as the descriptions proceeded.

Zombies, on the other hand, grew taller. Their nails grew three or more inches and were razor sharp. They turn leaner than the host. Their nose melts and disappears, getting replaced by larger holes that stuck flat on the face. This allowed the Zombies to have a better sense of smell, contrary to original misleading beliefs that had been spreading.

Zombies were also found to have red eyes. Their eyelids closed sideways from left to right on the left eye and from right to left on the right. This was because the Zombies, as opposed to humans, did not go out in the day time or when the light was present. The red eyes were theorized to be similar to night vision, allowing the Zombies to see things clearly and far away in the darkest darkness. Other scientists estimated it was infrared or a combination of both? These were all the features the Z did not possess.

The footage continued on the screens, respectively. Children all around the world were clung closer to their parents. It was indeed a horror movie come true.

The ears of a Zombie were smaller, the news continued, which diminished their sense of hearing. It was believed that the Zombies relied on sight and smell as the principal to find targets; humans. Neither the Z nor the Zombies reacted to noise regardless of how loud it was. They appeared to be completely deaf.

The most important question that everybody had been waiting for was not answered so far. It was on everybody's lips, but the scientists closed their reporting as soon as they relayed what they relayed. The remaining question hung invisibly in the air: "How do you kill them?"

***

The precautions were spread globally, no leaving home during the night time. Everybody carried a precautionary weapon in hand: some rod or hockey stick or baseball bat. For the nighttime, instructions were to keep from using running water (whichever rare places still had them), electricity (to remain in the dark), and use living animals like dogs and cats as bait if a Z or a Zombie found someone. After busying the creature, should they run?

The 20% of humans in the cities, and even the animals, that were alive were those with resilient immune systems. Most of the surviving sentient beings were in hiding, whether inside their homes or on the streets. The number who were opting for the latter were growing, though. At a rapid pace, the two kinds of creatures, especially the Z's, were silently invading homes, especially during the daylight.

Within the next month, half of the surviving human population was gone in the US, among which were the immune ones. It left around 10% of the human survivors overall. The majority of them were in the city who either had immunity to COVID-19 or didn't follow the rules. These were the Wolves that hid in Sheep's clothing. They were no longer wearing masks now, nor were they being reinforced.

These survivors usually lost at least one family member. Some were the lone survivors, and that's how they took on the streets. One individual or group would meet another, and after forming a trust, would become a part of the small clan.

The remaining few Sheep still did not change their ways. They decided to stay and wait for "Help" from the same government that initiated that catastrophe they were going through. They did not leave their homes.

Some of those that had full immunity against the COVID-19 did not die if they escaped Z or a Zombie after a single bite. But after enough bites, even they gave in. It was either due to the pain or the intensity of the spreading virus.

Sometimes, as many as 50 Z's could try to feed on a person brought down, according to a person's health. It was similar to watching a puppy or a kitten feed on their mothers' nipples. There would be more puppies than nipples, and while some would have to wait for the leftovers, others would tug and squirm to make room.

And it was in this that the scientist discovered one secret to how these creatures can be killed.

***

They appeared on the news channels again after a piece of breaking news was announced. Those who were alone or in groups on the streets tuned in on their radios.

If one or more Z's were to bite and eat some of the flesh or blood from an immune person, they would grow weaker and die as soon as the flesh hit the back of their throat. The human flesh with immunity was a weapon against them.

The person with immunity could survive with around 3 Z bites, depending on their health and location of the bite. If the jugular vein or a sensitive artery and the brain were bit, the person was more likely to die, especially if no one came to their aid. Yet if they were bitten by a Z on parts such as the hand or a finger, they could be saved and it would kill off the Z.

When those with the immunity were killed, the scientists reported that the body left behind could kill hundreds of Zs.

The survivors made notes and only felt some half-hearted rejoice. There has to be some other way to kill them too, they thought. Some of them who had encountered a Z or Zombie had tried giving them a bodily beating, but the creatures were numb to the pain. Even piercing the heart did not work.

The news continued and explained that this immunity weapon did not work against Zombies. They would not die as a Z did. Instead, they will quit feeding on the person and leave immediately to seek another human food source that was not naturally immune. These Zombies could alert the other Zombies not to pursue that immune person as a food source.

Zombies do possess superior intelligence to the Z. For the Z is similar to how humans in the past had pets like a cat or dog. In many ways, this is the best explanation of the relationship between the Zombies and the Z. The Zombie is the Master, and the Z is the Pet.

It was known that Zombies, for some unknown reason, do not like the sun. Scientists solved this mystery too. It was found that direct ULV Sunlight Rays were very deadly to Zombies. For this reason, they acquired shelter to rest or sleep, for which they need maximum darkness when the sun is out.

The scientist explained that even the slightest amount of light for the Zombies is like a parent trying to sleep with a waling baby in the room. Like humans, Zombies needed rest, and sleeping is the only way to rest for them.

The Z, on the other hand, worked non-stop until they were killed. The scientists admit they have not yet known how long Zombies and Z can go on without food. Their life span, too, remained a mystery thus far.

***

There were certain discoveries that the survivors, too, had made. Zombies did not like areas that exceeded 100 degrees or hotter at day or night. One group found this out as they camped and noticed with night vision binoculars how a Zombie could not sleep in a pitch dark environment. It writhed, and eventually, they figured it was due to extreme heat. The reason was unknown, but this pattern was confirmed by several other groups too.

When the surviving groups tracked on these Zombies, they were discovered to resist hot areas. With their growling sounds, they gather Z's around; they too are perturbed 100 degrees heat. Yet they hunt and collect flesh and blood for them, for they are subjugated after all.

Z and Zombies that transform in places like Las Vegas and Phoenix suffer the most. Countries Worldwide, such as those in the Middle East and South Asia, are relatively safer with their extreme summer heat.

Similarly, groups in Boston and Seattle discovered that both Zombies and Z could not withstand cold either. Both Zombies and Zs do not live, hunt, or reside in these areas. They migrate to moderately warm temperatures only.

***

All this information was given to Matthew right after the documentary about the past. The latest of the latest developments of the time these were. The boy who had lost two siblings to Zombies and Z's wiped his nose and looked up to the woman and man in the room.

"It's about time that I ask now, why am I here?"

Chapter 8
When

20th December 2026, the day when the Z transformations had first started, was soon to bring an end to a tradition.

The havoc and city-wide panic only wreaked havoc within the next five days. That was the last year when the humans of earth celebrated Christmas. How could they celebrate after all? The shops and stores were all announced closed. Decorations around the many cities all appeared as if abandoned midway. The streets were near to empty, seeming as bleak as the future. Little did people know that Christmases were to become extinct.

Everywhere on the streets were the beds of white; snow. Even though in these cities that were freezing cold, the Z's did emerge, they, along with the more evolved Zombies hit some type of hibernation. The majority of the people had hidden in their homes. The people would watch the number of survivors, which was 2 people in every 10, and even that figure started to drop away. Like street décor, the streets were spread out by eaten up human carcasses.

Rather than gather all the bodies and bury or burn the body, the survivors would skip through and learn exactly what they needed to do. The homeless ones immediately began to "claim" owned and abandoned residences. These were the houses that were now deserted or whose previous occupant had, either via death or self-exile by the people as I talked them into leaving the estate.

The strongest were among a few of the survivors who lived in their mansions and owned property. They isolated themselves into their separate rooms and waited for the hell to pass. Some had not put a cork on their ambitions for riches, thus, they would sometimes sneak out.

Some individuals adopted to the ever more intense anarchy more deeply. Those who had nothing or had lost all started to take over the homes of those who had left. Other opportunists who were more savage groups did not shy away from removing the former occupants from their own property. Had they only known that the majority of the two groups who usurped and were forced to leave would meet their deaths when the temperature would rise again. Those who willfully left with a destination in mind were among the most better off. Especially because they had a burning desire to survive, no matter what happened. They left with all the preparation. Many of these were city Wolves, who would be delighted to find another person to join them, forming groups. This practice became a commonality in both the hot regions and the cold.

The freezing temperatures helped many, but the more moderated regions saw a spike in zombie virus cases. These were people from places like Phoenix, San Diego, Las Vegas. The height of the hazard was at the highest here. Many survivors resolved to migrate to freezing cold places such as the Rocky Mountains in Colorado and Utah.

Those that remained left behind had one thing in common with those surviving in the wild; both feared Zombies the most. The Zombies had grown to be immensely hungry. By January 1, 2027, the population of mankind stood at 2.8 billion worldwide. In a week, nearly 4.8 billion people had either transformed, were transforming, or dead.

Nearly one-third of the World's population was gone, and hopes for population growth remained stark for many. Birth rates in the major cities had declined by nearly 86%. It was only the villages and small towns experienced normal rates of birthing and lifestyle.

The majority of worldwide regions with radically cold temperatures amounted to 1 billion. These Z's and Zombies were waiting for Warm Weather even while hibernating. Once they were to warm up, it was hoped through the radio that the majority of the human groups would have to place safe to survive.

The groups of people that would meet and integrate would have a good time sharing experiences and loss. These stories belonged more to those who had come from warm regions. Those from cold regions had experienced violence at the hands of humans only, while the warm region ones had seen catastrophes brought by Z's and Zombies.

Such heart to hearts built solidarity among groups. Many would get inspired after sharing and some would form sub-groups to scout for survivors on the streets, especially since their loved ones were gone.

In the beginning, most of the groups didn't mind that others wanted to join. They actually embraced it and allowed people regardless of what they brought in, for there was strength in numbers. Then, they started to observe the dark side of trusting humanity too much.

Among the ones they would take in were also people that would steal resources gathered by the group, even murder for them if they had to. These were the Sheep in Wolves clothing, playing out their animosity. This caused many of the city Wolves to tighten their initiation procedures. Most of the people were approved because they qualified as innocent and desperately needed support. Many had to be disenfranchised that there was no 'home' to return to, as they had been expecting.

They had to reject some members too. A few bad eggs would be found now and then, with questionable intents and morals. Sometimes the recruiters only went on their hunches when they refused. Other times they consulted among themselves to resolve that they had actually found an imposter, a Sheep in Wolf's clothing.

Many travelers were already grouped and yet merged two groups to sometimes form a small community-like environment. Some of these travelers were family members, who had either survived intact or lost at least one of their members.

Some of the groups traveled with keeping their destinations in mind. Most of these journeys were planned to where the Wolves lived. The Wolves had become the most reverent figures by then for the City Wolves. It was because they put heritage before all else and did not give in to conformist ideologies by the government. That's why they had been living a spiritual existence. Many of the Wolves lived in remote locations and were farmers, ranchers, etc. These were places that had 50,000 or lesser people who were not following any of the COVID 19 rules and requirements.

The Wolves rarely found the opportunity to fight or mob, yet they stored their weapons and bullets securely. It was something that the City Wolves and survivor Sheep could use once they would reach them – or if they would.

Could they know whether the Wolves would help them survive the Z and Zombie virus, which they had no contribution in creating? Only time and travel would tell.

Chapter 9
The 1%

Tucked away in their high castles, lavish and prim, each a Wayne Mansion of its own, were the 1% of the world. The routine included feasts and never-ending luxury. Business meetings, high-teas and parties, and whatnot. Their fortune-costing closets, diamond-encrusted doors, and walls, vintage-wine breaths had them consumed.

They did not know what their actions were going to amount to.

This was the life of the 1% who reveled in the success of having created a new society. Their success in making the binary of socioeconomic status among humankind called among them for a party, scheduled on Christmas night. Many were organized by the filthiest of the filthy rich at their places but little did they know, they had created monsters that would interrupt their celebrations.

Most of the families of the 1% were also planning on celebrating Christmas and joining the other elites. The Christmas day for the rich typically meant for their children the one day they would rise early, anticipating what the Santa Claus delivered under the Christmas tree. The guests were all preparing to fly to their hosts.

The children of the most powerful were thrilled to celebrate Christmas. The World around them was crumbling and falling apart, more so for the past five days, but none had learned about it yet. Such is the bliss of ignorance, especially when you are on cloud 9.

When one learned about it through their security protocol teams, the news spread like wildfire via call or text. They had been so out of tune with the 'anarchy' of the real world that they had stopped viewing the monitors. Now, they had no choice.

In the background were the delighted forms of their children, unwrapping the numerous presents; the foreground saw the elites fidgeting, terrified and incredulous.

"What bonkers fantasy is this? How could there come into existence such a creature as Z?" they would say. One by one, each of the elites canceled their plans for the Christmas party.

They went on the web and saws footages of the Z's gone pandemic. They attacked humans only, feasted on them while they were still alive.

One of the children innocently approached their fathers, asking, "What did Santa get you this year, Dad?" Neither of them could pronounce the gift they had received. The GIFT, being the death of soon-to-be billions, turning the surviving cities into slaughterhouses with carcasses lying out in the open. A portion of the 1% was fearful, regretting what they had done to humanity.

The majority of the 1% wealthiest people in the world lived in New York City, Los Angeles, and Miami. The county with the highest average income and the densest population of 1 percent resided in Teton, Wyoming. It was designed as the heaven on earth, attracting the world's wealthiest individuals such as Saudi Prince Alwaleed bin Talal.

The news came out after weeks that the Z's are hitting LA and Miami the hardest because of the warmer weather, but it was a bit too late. Even the extravagant wealth and resources of some of the 1% abiding there could not save them from the Z and Zombie attacks.

The survivors, however, left for Teton. These included Former Vice President Dick Cheney and the world's richest woman Christy Walton. John Frankly Mars, Chairman of the candy company Mars, Inc. all switched to Teton and called it home. Gus the largest Weed dispensaries owner, Denny, the computer genius, and several others of the top 1% returned to their already-established residences in Teton, Wyoming.

Wyoming was perfect for this pandemic since it had harsh winters. They were safest there, for the additional fact that residents of Teton had not worn masks for years. Regardless, among the surviving 1% grew the need to protect their wealth and numbers.

A hyper-virtual meeting was decided and set with the help of the most advanced technology. It allowed for the millions among the 1% to meet, and not for any celebration nor any party. They met to discuss the new status quo... but left with having created an instant division amongst themselves. This is how three groups broke out among the 1% of the world.

The first Group of the 1% included the cream of the crop; those that had five generations or greater of family representation as 1% members. All that was part of this group had maintained and augmented their wealth for 200 years or longer. Since they had the longest tenure, they believed they should be in control of the 1%, and executive powers in all matters.

Having been self-contained and full of themselves had a pathological effect on this group. The carnage, death, and destruction of man, caused by their actions generated nothing but indifference among them. They were in fact in favor to allow the barbarity to continue and were not willing to help.

Their egos were inflated beyond all inflatables. They thought they had every reason to, for they owned almost everything in the world. A number of the other 1% worked under them.

After a few of them gave their speeches, voting was opened to select a leader. However, each and everyone voted for themselves to lead. No leader was chosen, yet they were all leaders of their own agendas.

After their opening, the second group, including those that were recently inducted into the 1% and were not members via past generations, broke their silence. They had accomplished the feat within the last 3-30 years, and their source of pride was being self-made, rather than having inherited. They were not impressed by members of the first group, the old guard, who were born into wealth. They did not achieve the 1% status on their own, rather were eating the labors of their Great, Great, Great Grandparents, or relatives. That's what they would pass on to their future generations.

With their feet more grounded, most of these members were much more understanding of the masses. Before being in the 1% the majority of these were poor, middle-class hustlers. Some who did have wealth had pennies compared to what they now had. This group forwarded a stance of empathy and was more willing to work together for common goals than carrying forth indifferently.

Their addresses were informed by a feeling of guilt for the events that were happening. "In our pursuit of furthering our gains, we had not expected the rest of the world would get so crushed and doomed by our actions…"

But it soon turned out that not all who were part of the Second Group were in favor of the 'we' categorization. A few of them interjected saying they did agree with the first group. "The events that are happening, the masses that the Z's are killing is indeed beneficial for us. If we think about it, the results would ensure a healthy planet and complete dominance of only the 1% for the next several centuries or longer. This means no slum, only us."

Despite their stance, the First Group did not sympathize with these rebels. It had to do with their relatively inferior status.

The Third Group were the most arrogant and stubborn of the lot, so much that they refused to be part of any group. They refused any grouping and were concerned with things that personally affected only them... similar to those in the first group.

However, their stance differentiated in the belief that individually, they knew what should be done. They verbalized, "It would be best only if I were in charge." "Fortune is rooted in individual selfish concern," one of them said. It reflected immense ego, that too without even having the highest amount of power.

Their God complex was such that they looked down on even the remaining 1% as pests. Even those of the 1st group were not nearly as stubborn. They at least agreed to communicate and bring matters up for discussion. Yet this 3rd group didn't need any discussions because they knew what was best for everyone.

This group of the 1% pronounced that what was happening was the will of God. And so they lectured on fate and their 'every man for himself' ideology. This had countless members quit the meeting in rage, and thus, the dispute rose to such extremes that among them spread the rumor of two wars. One war against the Z's and Zombies, and the other against the divided 1%.

After the meeting, all of the 1% tightened their security. They also ensured their stock of weapons was abundant. The houses that some of them lived in may have been in warmer temperatures, but they had the best home security and state of the art home protection. Once they figured that God himself could not harm them, given their security, only then did they sigh a breath of relief.

Little did they know, their arrogance and hubris were to make them the first of the 1% group to be destroyed completely. They only cared for their own selves. Some even disregarded their families for the sake of their survival. What they had coming was what they deserved... As week three started since the first sightings of the Z, the 1% noticed the onset of zombies. The news reports aroused further panic. Creatures more deadly than Z's who could see even at night? The third group of the 1% thought these were demons from hell itself.

Meanwhile, the second group had been learning about the sufferings of the masses. While many amongst them did nothing, some set out to work together and to help whatever human life they encountered, regardless of their association.

The Second Group took it upon themselves to save, recover, and transfer any and all survivors they encountered per each shift. They set out with their massive security protocol and SEAL teams. As a result, tens of thousands were saved and sent to areas that didn't have any Z's or Zombies at that time. They had given out of their own hoarded resources to enable the survivors to sustain. Those that were saved cried out of gratitude and deemed them as guardian angels. These survivors were sent to Ranches, Farms, and places where it would be important to continue to grow food and have the resources. That was where the Wolves lived, who cautiously let the survivors in.

In Atlanta too, two Texans belonging to the second group did a similar thing. They saved a few thousand and took them to a safe and secure place. Whatever arsenal of weapons they had was entrusted to the masses. The 99% were happy to be tasked with being trained in, building, and assembling guns, rifles, and assault weapons. Some members also learned how to make and manufacture bullets.

The 1% was not doing this out of pure selflessness. After all, having enough bullets for the weapons and plenty of ammunition would be of future importance. It would be needed for the two battles. As to which of these two battles would begin first, this was the heated question as events unfolded, not just in the USA but worldwide.

The Zombies eventually adapted and discovered that plenty of humans were living where the lights were shining at night. They sent countless numbers of Z's for the houses were more like fortresses. Eventually, there turned out to be more Zs than some of the 1% and their security alike had bullets. This pattern started across the world. Largely, mysteriously, the members from the Third Group were at the forefront of the death toll. All that the army of Z's and Zombies needed was an opportunity for a breach. Once they got that, it was a matter of time before they would break-in and the place would become overrun with Z's and Zombies. Karma found those who represented only themselves receive the worst of it in this manner. Given how horribly they had treated those that protected and served under them, these people who worked under them thought they had had enough. They were to no longer bear any mistreatment, torment, or threats. Without any notice, the security guards, chefs, butlers, etc. all quit. Some, as they were departing, made sure that the gates were left unlocked to allow the Z and Zombie entry. This was the fate of the Third Group. After two months, almost none belonging to the Third Group remained alive.

Some other 1% escaped the breaches and found containment in a secure location. It was a part of their contingency plan. Some of them had enough supplies to last up to 20 years, others up to 2 years, and yet another batch about 6 months. Yet, the question was, how long could these individuals last being locked up? Living alone in a confined space was bound to make them go insane. Especially after their trauma of losing all their possessions and family members. A number of them could not endure for as long as a single week and resolved to commit suicide. The world's population was lowering to levels not seen since the 1700s. Plenty of the Major Cities such as New York, Chicago, Detroit to name a few were still frozen, but only for the time being. Once it warmed up, the human death rate was expected and predicted to rise.

Some of that 1% who had locked themselves up did realize the futility of it and escaped. They chose to be out in the open on their own and face whatever came, but with tears in their eyes. After all their scheming and manipulation through misuse of power, how ironic that they ended up as the most vulnerable. Unlike the masses, they were not street-smart and had never known rock bottom, which they were now subjected to.

For some of the 1% which did survive in the warmer locations which were few from the 1% lot to set out of their shells and landscape of riches. Dressed in poor people's clothes, stealing from their staff, they set out individually for the roads. All had packed weapons, most were strapped with more than their own weight. Their steps hit the snow, sand, and rocky terrains that they used to scoff at as the common man's land. Now they have to adjust and learn how to fit in as they walked along on it. Not two months ago could they have imagined this would happen to them.

They knew well enough now that getting accepted into the group of the masses, which means their worst former enemies, Wolves, or the other 1% rivals, would cost their ego. But after all, they had lost, their previous power, prestige, riches, they did not see the point of conceiving that 1%'s ego... They knew well that alone was more painful than having to seek help from the other survivors.

They decided to alter their demeanor, profiles as well as their names as well as their backstories. To be accepted, they had to disguise as an ordinary person. But that meant surviving on malnourished diets and extreme temperatures. Would they be able to fit in? How will they adjust from going to the top to the bottom?

The evolution of human strata had gone from multiple classes to two classes and now to simply one. Even within the 1%, only one group had survived, the second group of the 1% was willing to help all mankind.

Not all those among the surviving 1% had taken out on the streets. Some still hid in their homes, some were locked in contingency hatches with plenty of resources. They had a life trajectory of their own to follow.

What was to become of them?

Chapter 10
The Year 2027

The year 2027 saw more than half the world in locations that were not experiencing the white freezing-cold winters - no glaciers along with the water bodies, no snowstorms, and avalanches. It was in such a location that groups of scientists had camped. They analyzed vital information for the 1% after creating two new species, Z and Zombie. Part of their project was to gather footage and create data based on the transformations led by the new world carnage and death.

The scientists also ensured that more communication channels were opening up for survivors. They worked on technology that allowed survivor groups, such as the one in Teton, to review both live and recorded film footage. Given that the smart minds were not only among the scientists, the survivor groups also made discoveries.

When a Zombie first bites certain people, they will not be further attacked by the Zombie; instead would be left alone. The scientists acquired full access to live video feeds by tapping into the security cameras, private and public, still operating. Certain major cities did have most of the operating cameras working. For the cities and areas where working cameras or recording devices were not operational were soon introduced with satellite recording from space.

They learned when the Z first appeared that certain people, when bitten by one of the Z, resulted in the Z dying in a matter of moments. The person who was being attacked, on the other hand, was capable of surviving. The scientists noted this furiously in their books and brainstormed amongst them in the dimly-lit labs. The scientists' biggest concern was what those people had that killed Z if that person were bitten. They were curious about the long-term side effects of the Zombie bite.

When the scientists began communicating with the survivors, they extended this investigation query to them. After studying dozens of live and recorded footage of people killing Z by being bitten and otherwise individuals, they noticed that while the pattern pertained with the Z, Zombies, on the other hand, did not pay any heed to such human that was immune to them. It was as if these people did not exist in the eyes of the Zombies.

The group in Teton confirmed this and shared the knowledge with others worldwide. Other groups in different locations began to study this finding and assigned more groups to learn of why a Z would die, yet Zombies didn't even notice those immune individuals. With more eyes working, studying, and thinking about the feeds, the probability would eventually show, hoped the scientists.

That did turn out to be the case. A woman named Aspyn Tayler was the first to confirm from footage that a Zombie will not bite or attack humans, which can kill a Z, especially if they had been bitten by Z. These are the only individuals which a Zombie will not bite, attack, or seek out.

Aspyn Tayler learned two things. First, Zombies will only bite those that have yet to be bitten and have a natural antivirus in their systems. When a Zombie bit these individuals, the Zombie did not die; instead, the people got sick and had to leave instantly if they survived. While if a Z bit these people with the natural antivirus, the Z would die.

Aspyn also discovered that these people with the antivirus bitten by Z's developed something smell-wise or sight-wise, making them invisible to the Zombies. Zombies could surround these individuals, yet they would completely ignore them because a Z previously bit them.

This discovery by Aspyn was vital, a cause for worldwide celebration. It proved that mankind had a natural defense against the Z Virus. Teams of scientists were dispatched to the more densely-populated cities with people that had the antiviral gene. The aim was to create effective anti-viruses by replicating the genetic structure and possibly also create weapons to use against the Z and Zombies.

And so with changing paradigms, humans with proven, natural antivirus identified became the most important people alive. They attained more importance than the scattered 1%. These were the individuals who held the key to man having any chance of survival from the COVID-26, the Zombie Virus.

People that were conditionally invisible to the Zombies with natural antiviruses were sought using cameras and satellites. The scientists paired up with remained armed forces to ransack them. To find what they had required that these people be brought back to Teton and investigated in the superlabs to seek what made them who they were. The white-coated scientists aided by armed forces set out at the break of day and returned from their search before the sunset. The scientists were not solely dependent on antiviral humans. They had learned a while ago that the Zombies only went out when it was night time. Hence, using that knowledge, a group that had been assigned the duty of producing anti-Zombie equipment ended up creating a powerful flashlight beam that contained various spectrums of light present when the sun was out. It was hoped to work at least as a Zombie-repellant if it would not kill them.

Scientists were curious to see what would happen if the Zombies were exposed to this artificial light. They had yet to encounter a Zombie to test it.

The people with antiviruses, when sought out, would usually panic before the team of scientists and armed men. But the teams brought with them white flags that they would wave, which always led to a peaceful transition. In the end, those people who were found and gave their consent would be taken to Teton.

These operations of 'Seek and Relocate' were happening in the cities that were warm and with high Z and Zombie hazards. The teams would go out and find survivors other than their targets, begging them to save them too. It would be an impossible task to remove all the remaining survivors during that first mission, especially with the Z's being out who never rested. So the teams would have to tell them instead to "Leave the city immediately and head to [a resourceful location] for future pick up. Either that or at the very least go where it is cold or freezing."

Some would instantly leave and begin to go to the instructed location. Others would leave seeking to go where it was cold and still freezing. Then there would be others who remained behind, more of the Wolfish nature who did not believe in authorities' word. They knew that help would arrive only for those whom the teams were seeking.

Most of those that were being sought were found and located. Some did not wish to leave, for they had other people relying on them, whom they wanted to stay with. They were willing to go if those people could come along. Yet the others could not be allowed to join at that time. Promises could be made only for future rescues, but not the present. Hence, a fraction of immune humans left behind by choice. With the approach of twilight, the second wave of helicopters would arrive to dispatch the second group. They were those that were armed with powerful flashlights, weapons, and medical equipment. This group was assigned two missions. First, finding those on the list that have yet to be found and relocated, and the second was to field test, record the nocturnal flashlight weapon results.

The freshly arrived second group had taken notes from surveillance and knew of possible Zombie hideouts. These were usually locations with high Z populations during the day time. In locations where power had permanently gone out, satellites had been watching, and even drones were filming events as they happened in real-time.

The teams knew that much was at stake, for soon, most of the world would be warming up with the onset of spring. This was a high time for all kinds of experimentation. Every second was a second closer to when it would no longer be freezing in the Northern Part of the USA, Canada, and other relatively arctic regions in the upper Northern Hemisphere of the World.

The weather was continuing to warm up for the next wave of terror at places that were still frozen. Even in hibernation, it seemed like the Z's and Zombies were waiting to colonize the freezing regions. The scientists knew that mankind's greatest threat, the COVID _26_, the Zombie virus, could mean extinction. It could kill off even more people, further lowering the worldwide population of all of humanity to the lowest in nearly a thousand years. During the nighttime missions, some groups would succeed, some would fail, many would die – and would be termed as martyrs. They knew what they had signed up for, knew they were the only hope for mankind to have a fighting chance.

The armed teams successfully found locations such as underground tunnels or large abandoned buildings during the nocturnal hours where the Zombies hid. Other places like schools, hospitals, airport terminals, shopping malls, places that previously allowed thousands to gather were some of the locations that were confirmed to be where the Zombies remained hidden.

The second teams would penetrate by first killing off the Z's that were guarding these entries. They would proceed into the buildings with the body cameras as the scientists observed them from their labs. During the early operations, they discovered that the flashlight was not powerful enough to kill the Zombies, but it was more than a Zombie-repellant. It caused what appeared to be an enormous amount of pain in the Zombies.

However, when the groups were able to force a Zombie in the direct sunlight after the wee hours of dawn, it would indeed kill the Zombies that survived the night. The scientists who were watching knew that some spectrum of light, possibly a spectrum not yet discovered or known, was missing from the weapon. Of course, that was the spectrum of light that was most needed to make the weapon deadly. Their experimentations continued.

Once enough humans with natural antiviruses were secured, the final mission for the first team was to bring back at least one dead Zombie and Z. The scientists were going to dissect and experiment on Zombie and Z corpses to learn more of the biological facts of these two new species. This meant DNA samples, blood, and other fluids or such particular to Zombies or Z's.

Their priority was alive Zombies, and if not alive, they required at least several corpses of both Zombies and Z's. That way, autopsies could be done to learn more of Man's greatest and most deadly enemy. It was thought that the second team would have to be merged with the first for this mission. As a better precaution, the humans that were immune tagged along with the teams. Each of them had one of their body parts bandaged from being bitten by a Zombie or Z. This mission resulted in a few of the Z's being captured alive and transported back. It was known that a lot of the men and women on this mission would not see the dawn of the new day, for they would be killed. However, the majority that entered the Zombie hideouts survived, thanks to following the protocol prescribed.

Some lives were lost due to the light weapon not affecting the Z's, which was a novel discovery. Their surprisingly piercing bites would tear through the armors; Z-specific weapons had to be used on them.

The story's successful side was that three live Zombies were captured and placed in a sealed container. It was a carefully-designed metallic prison that did not allow any light for the long transportation back to Teton, Wyoming. These three Zombies were precisely what the Scientists required for testing and experiments and were the only hope at the cost of many lives lost.

***

When morning would break out in camps at the frontier of the country, or fringes of the country, many of those who had been earlier classified as Sheep and the Wolves would wake up amongst each other. Some would go out to gather water. Another merged group would scout for resources and people. They knew that if they had to survive, they had to do it together as one. The 1% and the governments were no longer in control, though they were a covert part of these camps now. The Zombies and the Z had become the dominant species. Most of the 1% had seen their fall. governments no longer existed, only anarchy. All this happened before the Springtime of 2027.

The second most dominant group was, of course, the Wolves. They had always been ahead of the 1% and the Sheep. Their farsightedness of many years had proven useful since they had ever been stockpiling on ammunition, guns, weapons, food, water, and even medical supplies. The stockpile was to be used in the war against the 1% and the governments; the Wolves had earlier thought. Instead, it was being used against the Zs and the Zombies.

***

The weather was turning warmer in places. The heavy jackets and padded layers of clothes were coming off from the survivors. It was during these times that the counterstrikes and retrieval missions titled 'Healthy Humans' took place. The teams sent this time had three different goals now. The first was to extract all humans that did not have any signs or symptoms of the COVID-26, the Zombie Virus. However, the decision of a person who did not want to be 'saved' by being extracted and moved to a safe location was instructed to be honored. The terms of such missions were interesting for the Wolves, who could not place the scientists and armed forces.

These survivors, especially those who had been Sheep, would learn from Wolves how to farm and garden. They would take care of the surviving cattle and help with the manufacturing of weapons and ammunition in the endangered times.

The second mission was to kill and destroy all the Zs and Zombies in the stages of hibernation, which had yet to transform fully. Drones had picked up on places they were hiding in still-freezing places, which the teams would raid. Any other Z and Zombie encountered in the city was to be killed. If possible, the capture of more live Zombies was encouraged as the scientists had exhausted their earlier samples due to more failed testings than successful.

They had yet to explore what weapons could work to kill them the best. Other questions such as how long they could live without any food, i.e., human flesh, and what they can and cannot endure in extreme hot and cold temperatures.

Finally, the toughest of all was mission number four. It was to locate specific supplies. Supplies such as food, medicine, technology, weapons, materials, and any other needs were requested for survival.

"What is so difficult about these missions," one of the agents asked from a leading scientist in Teton.

"These are often the locations that are occupied by the Zombies during the day. Remember how the Zombies were occupying malls and other empty buildings? It is here where the supply of articles is most abundant… Which makes these most dangerous locations, especially since we do not have fatal weapons against Zombies, and they are likely to adapt to the Zombie Flashlights."

Another scientist continued, "This is why those teams involved in this fourth mission, would face the most difficult time of all."

The agents looked from one to another and gulped.

Chapter 11
The Safe Zones

Some scouts were returning from the frosted woods with small inconsistent sacks filled with food, medicine, other medical supplies, equipment, materials, tools, anything they could find. They came across a water carrier from another friendly camp they knew.

"Heading back to your Safe Zone?" the water-carrier asked, adjusting his container on his back. These kinds of conversations were common.

"Yeah, you to yours?" asked Gus, the once-largest owner of the weeds dispensary. The man from the 1% tribe had blended well with the survivors, adjusting his ways, including his accent.

"Yeah but, our group's kinda tripping, you know. For now, the zone is good, but we fear the end of winter."

"I wouldn't fear it if I were you. We haven't had a single issue except for some pussy-ass cases of theft at our Safe Zone. No issues with Zombies or Zs neither 'ccording to all the camps we've interacted with. I'd say we go on living the way we're living," Sebastian, who was one of the Wolves and the leader of the group, replied, only seriousness on his face.

The water-carrier nodded and moved on.

The camps had been careful to register themselves with particular Safe Zones, set in places with the longest Winters. There were 158 of them, which were built like communities with a semblance of society warehouses. Helipads were built into these locations, which could house several helicopters with sufficient resources to refuel them.

The Safe Zones also provided storage. The helicopters would return from the cities filled with teams, and supplies would be exchanged at the Safe Zones.

It was in these Zones where Zombies and Z, dead or alive, along with other items requested by teams, were transported to Teton. The Safe Zones are also places where those on missions return to, bonding with survivors in the city, transporting the ones who wanted to be relocated. The Zones were the go-to place for any kind of requirement.

It also serves as a place to rest and sleep. All those that stayed there had to play their part, though. Some preferred to play their role by preparing for the next mission when needed. Others went on scouting or rescue missions. Only the select few and the most trusted ones were kept for guarding and security duties, armed with top guns and armors. The vast majority of those are people that formerly served in the military,

Like a mini-city, there was an order and structure in place at Safe Zones. There were departments such as clinics for doctors, restaurants for cooks, and so on for maintenance and residential areas. Spread across the whole world, Safe Zones are the only places with some semblance of hope and unity for the remaining humanity.

The group led by Sebastian the Wolf walked across and came upon the road where they had parked their semi-trucks. The men guarding the trucks nodded in acknowledgment, and all of the survivors stepped in.

Because of the appalling state that the roads had been in since 2020, traveling by car was no longer possible. The overgrown trees, weeds, plants had invaded the asphalts. The bridges were all burned and were a huge risk to cross.

At the narrower lanes, motorcycles and some 4-wheelers were used, but that was not the need for this day. Mainly, though destroyed, the roads were broader, and the number of supplies was in plenitude. That was the reason Helicopters and Airplanes were preferred for larger missions and resource transport, especially when the distance amounted to hundreds or thousands of miles away.

It was possible to travel on foot too, of course, if required and needed. Sometimes, horses could be utilized too. These vehicles favored speed, but not the number of resources to be carried. All these vehicles were kept in garages inside Safe Zones, which were usually used for recon and patrol.

Among Sebastian's group that headed out into the woods were also hunters. They had formerly been Wolves and were trained in securing fresh meat supplies from rabbits to deers and ***other creatures of the forest.***

Most of the rescue missions that took place, like the one where the water-carrier's group had headed out for, usually rescued Sheep survivors. They would be brought to the closest Safe Zones near their area of rescue, treated, fed, and so on.

At first, most of them feel grateful. Others grow sad for the people they leave behind or the trauma they bear. There were also among those that were angry and secretly patronized their rescuers.

Some of the rescued Sheep on that particular mission, instead, felt bothered in all rescue missions. Not only would their rescuers not be wearing any mask, they too would not be allowed to wear one either.

"This is preposterous!" one of the rescued people said after holding it in.

The rescuers looked at them, and having been used to this behavior, would look away from them. Some of them were converts too, former Sheep, so they knew that once they also felt the same way.

"You're not allowing any masks, all of us are cramped here with no social distancing. Do you want to get us killed?"

Another more timid Sheep pointed out to their guns. "You guys have weapons too. This is just so savage."

One of the Wolves, who was by then a good friend with a Sheep, looked at his friend mockingly. His friend was embarrassed that he once used to be like that. The Sheep would stop complaining by themselves, for they were never conditioned to do anything safe for that.

Some of those that would be angry were the 1%, having lost all that they had made them bitter. Other than that, they were not used to winters, so they would be trembling sick with a cold. Sometimes they were found alone, but most of the time, they hid with the Sheep. Given that the Sheep were easily recognized by the Wolves, who were usually the rescuers, the 1% were automatically classified as one of them, like on this particular mission. Thus, they were never found out, even despite their tantrums, complaining about silly nothings.

It had been easier for them to fool the Sheep and bribed them with plenty of weapons, firearms, guns, assault guns, and ammunition, which they lied came from dead Wolves or armed forces killed by Z's or Zombies.

The 1% in Sheep's clothes, which were not frustrated initially, would be angered and hurt in their pride as to how much the Sheep and Wolves had amassed. They also despised that the food, medicine, and other essential items were being sent to Teton, where the 1% were still residing.

What was left behind was a small percentage of stock, with only the illusion of an 'exchange' taking place.

From the moment they exited – those that chose to – and left the plane or helicopter, they follow as they were instructed. They were given two choices: Follow the group you arrived with or be detained immediately and then released outside the borders of the Safe Zone compound, never to return. Most would follow the group they arrived with. Others will choose to opt-out and be transported out beyond the barriers of the Safe Zone compound.

The hopes for recuperation for the new arrivals at the Safe Zone would come with Orientation sessions. That would begin immediately for the new arrivals at a Safe Zone.

Among those that remained, the vast majority would be led to the Orientation room. Once all the new arrivals were present and accounted for, the room would be darkened, and an old projection using tape reels would begin.

The audio in the water-carrier's Safe Zone was scratchy with interruptions, but the audience was glued. It had been five or so years since they viewed or witnessed any film or screen. For the most part, the audiences would typically be silent. However, a few of the former 1% members in Sheep's Clothing would react in some outrageous way, given how egotistical they had been. It would lead them to being discovered during the initial orientation.

With their ego acting as the downfall, these individuals would be given two choices.

"First: stay and ensure the lowest of all jobs. The bottom *1%* of all the jobs. You will work longer hours than all others, and harder than the remaining *99%*, only to get the minimum of quota-based resources in return. You will officially be the bottom *1%*, recognized by the Safe Zone and beyond."

This would make a lot of them squirm, scoff or snort. The survivors would immediately lay down the second option.

"If you refuse to do so, you will be taken 20 miles beyond the secure free zone compound and asked never to return."

Those with the largest egos would leave. Those who remained would face the karma they bred, taking the worse cleaning jobs and serving under the Wolves and Sheep. Gus was not one of them. He did not have to select either of the two options, for he was smart enough to stay shut during his

Orientation. ***Gus also cared for all humans and wanted to help and change what the 1% have created.***

From the Safe Zone, 80% or greater of arrivals would be transferred to a site for further testing and training, such as for agricultural produce. Other talents and skills would be evaluated, too.

Some would be sent to locations specializing in Medical and Technology, along with Science, which was the most challenging sector. The 80% of the transferred would become farmers, cooks, go into laundry services, maintenance, or become a part of armed forces that carried out missions 24/7. The war between the humans and Z's was a non-stop war, and with more cities than people and equipment, those that failed to fit in with the others or within their assigned group would become a soldier, a warrior for humankind.

That is also what happened with 95% of those that remained back in the Safe Zones during each transfer. A few became part of the internal maintenance of the safe zone: cooks, maintenance, cleaners, communications, for example. They were to be trained and then sent out to missions. Training took ten days, after which they had to carry out missions 12 hours per day for ten days in a row with two days off after the 10th day. This went on until they died.

Among the recruits, especially those without military or police training, the mortality rate was in the high 80's. With most of the Sheep, this was a sorry affair, as they were assigned either at the Main Operations in Teton or at one of the Safe Zones.

They had to understand the farce of wearing face masks and the importance of socializing. In the trying times, being close to others showing affection was encouraged. Every person was on a schedule and had to be responsible and do some service to earn and keep their place within the Safe Zone.

While for some, these Zones were a sanctuary, needless to say, to some of the Sheep, the free zone or Teton was a prison. Some of the Sheep would regroup at times and discuss amongst themselves things such as, "Have we gone from the frying pan to the fire? Those who control us, they are no better than the 1% or the failed governments they so preach us against?"

This would be the start of a gas spread on dried wood that only needed a match to start a fire. Tensions were raised like wildfire, for it was a rule of the Wolves where they did not have anything to do for fun except have sex.

All the movies had long been seen, all the songs listened to, and the books read. Vacations no longer existed because life required daily tasks. For those that battled and had missions, survival was the only thing on their mind.

Amidst these tensions came the time when Springtime began to approach towards the Northern Hemisphere. The missions to the city were forced to cease. This was agreed by Teton, for too many active Zombies and Z's were lurking.

Those who chose to remain behind in the cities became the Zombies' last food sources until only dogs and cats remained for the Z to feed on.

The occupants inside the Safe Zone started growing jittery around that time. They had too many supplies and weapons with little to no activities remaining to do. The feeling of being inside prison only started to grow, even for those that had thought of it as a sanctuary. The Sheep and the 1% felt like they were in an asylum as they were being bullied and ordered around by the ***Wolves*** for petty duties and tasks.

It was only a matter of time that the top 1%, now among the bottom 1%, ignited the fire for revolt among the Sheep inside the Safe Zones.

Chapter 12
The Encounter

Aldous peeked his head inside the empty room and was signaled by all the rest inside. He brought the last Sheep behind him and quietly shut the door.

"Nobody make any noise. We don't want the Wolves or the Almost-Wolves finding us in here," he said, sweat dripping and seriousness glaring in his eyes.

He passed his eyes across all the 30-some faces. Most of them were scared. Typical Sheep, Aldous thought within him.

In his past life, Nick Aldous was among the world's 1%, owning the biggest toiletry and liquid plumber companies in the world. The irony of fate that his new life had him mopping bathroom floors and cleaning out commodes. Hence he had cooked up a plan with some of the 1% connections in the Safe Zones he was around.

"You are the third batch I'm talking to, and by now, you all know why you're gathered here. All of you come from a civilized way of life. You have been respectable Sheep, done your duties, and bothered no one. No matter how tough it got, you stuck by what was necessary, protected yourselves with masks and gloves, and distancing.

"Being brought here has been the most humiliating and ridiculous thing ever. Like other former Sheep, the Wolves are looking to brainwash you too." He looked at his once-manicured fingernails and frowned at the dirt they'd gathered. Then he looked up at the faces, looking mortified now. His words were working.

"I don't see happy faces among any of us, but I see plenty of joy on them. They treat us like a joke, milk all out us like we're cows, and force us to do their dirty jobs. This hierarchy won't do. We are going to fight against them because I don't see any of us doing that for us."

Nick Aldous was aided by some 1% disguised as Sheep, all of whom continued the job of riling the Sheep up.

As the first riots began, a total of seven safe zones were under attack on the same day. The Wolves and their allies, having gotten complacent and did not see it coming. Was it a planned attack agreed upon by the seven different Safe

Zones? They could never tell, at least the few remaining ones, for the places were left with only a few survivors.

Three of the 7 Safe Zones were completely blown up, leaving only death in its wake. The other 4 had less than 20% survival rate between the Occupants and the Sheep.

The remaining 158 Safe Zones in the US had yet to have any riots or attacks. The Wolves and their allies replied by removing all new trainees, Sheep, and 1%, from training. They were kept far from weapons and explosives. All remaining Safe Zones and changes were immediately made to the primary operations.

The Sheep were bounded and handled roughly, gathered and huddled in locked chambers. This affected the rioting plans that were to follow in the other Safe Zones. They could not proceed further. While it adversely impacted the Sheep and the 1%, the Wolves themselves were not satisfied. The humans had again only done things to aid the Zombies.

The rioting armies had begun by effectively killing off all modes of communication first. So the handful that survived at the Safe Zones knew that help would not be on its way soon. They were no longer able to communicate with Teton or any other Safe Zones. They knew they were on their own, so the surviving Wolves and their allies, most of them injured, took to the road. Some took the 4 X 4 vehicles, which helped carry remaining supplies such as ammunition, medical supplies that they could gather along with some food. Others left on motorcycles with two or three people on it.

Out of the 7, only 4 Safe Zones at least had some survivors. Some of the groups had a destination in mind, such as checking on and seeking sanctuary in the closest nearby Safe Zones. Other groups did not have a destination, so they went with a few supplies their way. Most of them had lost their friends and the few remaining loved ones.

All groups, whether on foot or vehicles, stuck together pursuing their destinations.

The scarce amount of remaining fuel was reserved for the motorcycles largely. Hopes were that they could possibly locate a fuel source to bring for the bigger vehicles and stay available for the long journey of traveling to the nearest Safe Zone. They did locate some fuel at times, giving that group a few days' worth of gas supply. Some did not find fuel and would have to gather that they could carry and make the rest of the journey by walking.

Since all four of these groups did not have any communication, they were on their own and quite aware of being blind. Blind, without any drones flying or satellites surveilling. These had been available before, using which they could tell if Z, Zombies, or any danger lurked nearby. Now there was uncertainty. Could they survive if they were attacked and without the aid of communication and technology? Could they survive any hazardous encounters that may happen during these journeys?

Some groups on their scouting mission procured a satellite device. They eventually made contact, hoping on the other side were humans. Humans who did not wear masks, carried weapons, and offered aid and assistance towards the Free Zone survivors. That was exactly what they found. In exchange for that help, all weapons the survivors had with them had to be turned over to rescue others, protect food, and provide shelter. If they decided to leave, they would then receive the weapons they turned over.

The Free Zone survivors were distributed in four groups, each with its own leader.

After what happened in the riots, they were not going to trust their rescuers. Wherever they went, they bound and gagged those people that saved them, leaving their survival to fate. When asked, the reason would just be, "You know what just happened," referring to the riots.

Soon, word via oral communication got out among the groups and communities that were rescuing others. These were the local Wolves that had not interacted with outside society in decades.

Within a brief amount of time, the survivors who just arrived were now surrounded by the locals. For every survivor, there were eight or more locals. The locals also were well-armed and appeared to be experienced in handling weapons. Eventually, all four of the different groups in different locations were caught in similar situations while being completely unaware of their sync.

The rescuing communities gave the four groups the option of turning their weapons over. "We could kill you," they said, "but we are in need of good fighters, men and women both."

Only when they turned the weapons over as requested by the locals were they welcomed into their community.

Those that needed medical attention were taken care of immediately. The remaining would be treated to a meal or shower, or both. Some of the survivors were tense, even with all that was being offered. They spoke very little, only having a small chat, and always remained on guard.

Other surviving members would tell the locals of the recent events of why they were on the road, so they knew from where their loss of trust emerged. Some in the group listening were thankful that the free zone survivors no longer had their weapons, wondering if they did the right thing to let them in.

Some of the locals engaged with their stories. "Why were you taking Sheep...er city folk outta of the city?"

The survivors would respond, "It was our job and duty to save as many humans as possible. Not very different from you."

Two of the four local rescuer groups, having been Wolves in ostracized communities, had not known about the Zombies and Z until only recently. And so their biggest question was the same thing to all surviving groups, "How did this happen, these ZOMBIES and the other Z coming up?"

By this time, it was common knowledge to the survivors how the Z and Zombies were created. They were told about the creatures which they had not known, for they hadn't had any traveler in a long while. That's who they depended on for outside knowledge. These were the purest of the Wolves

"The Z appear Human-like," they were told, "and do not grow, yet they have blackness for eyes and small razor-like teeth." And so on, they told the locals all about the Z's and Zombies, including experimental vaccines, and the weaknesses and strengths of the two creatures. All that had been researched and known so far was relayed to the groups.

The Wolves were stunned to learn about them. They felt like they were reading from a fantasy dystopian sort of a book. They were then informed of the rescues and supply missions to the cities, along with killing and testing of as many Zombies and Z possible by the scientists and armed forces.

The Wolf groups asked, "If there's no government or the 1%, who is in charge now?"

This was one question to which all four groups provided different responses. Not a single survivor from the fallen Free Zones knew the right answer. The survivors were low-ranking individuals among the Wolves predominantly or the Sheep, who was not part of the riots. They were going on missions; some who survived were cooks, some were in charge of maintenance.

It was agreed by all four of these different groups of Wolves and Survivors that Zombies and Z would need to be controlled and then eliminated. This was a war between humankind and the infected. It would require all humans, young and old, those that can fire a gun or shoot a rifle to stand up to the Zombies and Z's.

After this was decided and agreed upon, those local Wolves went to nearby communities of Wolves, one by one. They shared the word about all that they learned about the new world order.

They were convinced that humans had to take back their right to lead this planet. The survivors of the Free Zone knew that these local Wolves would be far greater warriors than the Sheep and 1% they were attacked by. These Wolves were battle-ready and had been preparing for outside threats for this day for a long time.

They had not expected that this battle would not be against the government or the 1% for their rights. It had to be against a far greater threat, for all of mankind and man's future amidst the Zombie Virus, the **_COVID 26_**, creator of the Z and Zombies.

Once both sides mutually earned the trust, of the locals and the survivors, it was the right time for the four survivor groups to tell the locals of the secret signal.

"Create too large X's one red and one yellow on top of each other yet separate in an open area." This was a signal to Teton, which still had satellites, planes, and even drones passing above. Eventually, these two X's will be spotted, and help could then arrive.

True to their word, the two large X's were painted. The groups were indeed found after three days, and a week later, two helicopters arrived as they saw the four locations with the signal, the red and yellow X's from the survivors. The initial landing and first meeting were similar to how the Wolves first greeted the Free Zone Survivors of the cities.

As the two helicopters landed, a few of the locals stood near the helicopter landing zone. In a matter of moments, that number of locals would only continue to increase. One of the Free Zone survivors would stand nearby, and things would be more at ease when the Teton teams noticed them. The arriving team would then go directly to one or more of the Free Zone survivors since they were also part of the same operation and preferred to hear from these people first.

Even though the arriving teams would be outnumbered and outgunned, they would pose command, wishing to speak to those that had the same uniform as they were wearing. After they would talk with their trusted individuals and were convinced, the arriving crew commander would order for all to give up their arms and weapons as requested by the locals, the Wolves.

They would all gather, and as the helicopters would begin to quiet down, the questions would begin. At first, the discussions started unruly, where all were speaking and having their conversations.

Then the commander would make its way forward and demand to meet the person in charge.

One woman of the first of the four communities replied, "No one person is in charge, all of us are in charge. We here at ***Jackpot*** vote as a group and all of us have a voice." The Commander, not expecting this nor prepared, took a moment and introduced himself.

"I am Gus, the commander of this operation. We are here to assist you and help with anything we can and are capable of."

Some locals commented under their breath, "This sure looks and sounds like the government to me." Gus hears this and tells those that have gathered, "No, no more governments anywhere. I am part of a group of people that are trying to save mankind. Our home operations are in Teton, Wyoming and I am inviting your leader or leaders to join me and my team as we return our members whom you have taken care of back to Teton."

A local shout out, "What if we don't want to go with you, you going to try to force us?" Gus responded, "No, my friend, I am not here to force any of you. I was extending an invitation to invite a few of you to join me and my comrades to return with us. It's totally optional. Those that do accept my offer will be treated well and will be returned home, back here after you have met with those that lead our group in this war with the Zombies and Z."

After the first group was located and found, those back in Teton were better prepared for the next three groups. They were each soon discovered by the two Xs. Gus was also the leader on these remaining three correspondences and was much better prepared when they occurred.

The remaining three groups which had provided the X signal were found within a week. These meetings were much smoother than the first. Gus was successful in bringing a few members from each Wolf community to Teton.

At this time, the Zombies and Z in America greatly outnumbered all remaining humans worldwide. For every human being alive, there were at least 100 Z's and Zombies.

All four groups finally arrived along with the Wolves that joined them, all under Teton's same location. Those survivors that had their reunion caught up with the other groups and learned of the other Wolves and similar experiences they shared without knowing. The Wolves, too, realized that there were many other Wolves such as them. These Wolves all knew from what they had seen and learned that they were the purest among the Wolves, and the majority of those in Teton were not warriors like they were. Gus and the other leaders of Teton knew that this was true as well.

Teton did have more advanced weapons and those with military experience. But with all the missions they had been doing for the last several months, those with military experience had been dying during the missions, and those that hoped to replace the trained military were killed in action against the Zombies and Z. The Sheep could no longer be trusted with weapons to replace those who have died.

The people that can and will fight are those that are Wolves. And since these Wolves had been found, other Wolves also must still be alive. Probably also not be aware of the Zombies and Z's. This was indeed verified by the Wolves, that a large number of others pure Wolves had yet to be found by those in Teton or at the remaining Safe Zones.

The main objective then became to find these rural locations and small cities. Once they were located, a team made up of Teton, and some from the Wolves traveled together to inform and recruit the Wolves. Those from Teton would always allow and let the Wolves who were traveling with them on each of these trips to take the lead and be the first to tell those locals of all that they had discovered in the last several months. Being in Teton had also exposed them to Z's and Zombies kept captive for various experimentation. Most of those locals did not know about the new Virus COVID-26 and the Zombies and Z.

This news spread like wildfire in these distant and stealthy communities. Most rural populations were also informing and recruiting their neighboring communities. The Teton teams were surprised to find all the small towns and cities organized by Wolves that had yet to have any Zombies or Z.

Most communities had agreed to join in the battle. Some declined and were never to be bothered again, as per their instructions. There was no violence on any of these missions, all led by Gus, a hopeful man who would now at least be a chance for humankind to survive from becoming extinct.

Chapter 13
The Cities

The cities with large populations who had been under the control of the 1% had seen no one enter their borders for a few weeks. No longer were there any outsiders coming in; outsiders who were on a mission to find survivors and supplies, along with killing as many Z and Zombies they encountered. The Sheep and Sheep in Wolves' clothes who had given birth to the pandemic were the only occupants.

These occupants had been told they would be next to be transferred to a Safe Zone. They waited listlessly in their homes where everything was a wreck, surviving on the bare minimum. The outsiders could not carry out the rescues because none of the helicopters were free.

The command that there would be no more trips to the cities was a safety net against the risk and danger, especially after the fall of seven former Safe Zones being destroyed by the saved Sheep. The aid that had been coming in in the form of air-dropped packages guarded by troops had also ceased when the order was given. The Sheep, while they were naïve, were not necessarily fools. They knew that something was wrong. The groups of armed forces and scientists had been coming in to carry out missions in those 158 cities 24 hours a day, seven days a week. Now they had ceased suddenly. With that were left behind those that were securing the items, the rescuers and Z and Zombie-slayers. They were stuck in the cities with minimal amounts of ammunition. They soon came to be known as the forgotten.

Some groups of the forgotten knew what had happened. They would immediately leave that city and take a chance outside of the highly Z and Zombie populated locations. Other groups tried to set up a location near the common drop and pick-up locations, waiting for someone to return for them. Some groups would stay and continue to fight both the Z and Zombies and also take in any human they may encounter or find.

As the days turned into weeks, then the weeks into months, Summertime eventually came upon North America. Places that were once freezing or frozen with cold-weather began melting. It was the time everybody had feared. The time for Z and Zombie to all come alive in the Major Cities.

Humans that were alive wished they had left the city a long time ago when they watched the creatures crowd upon the streets. Those that were living provided the food source for the Zombies. Human populations continued to decrease Worldwide, heading towards extinction. In every city worldwide that was occupied by Zombies and Z dying become easier than living. It was not only the fear of Z and Zombies; they had no food either.

The only thing left for them to do was to seek out humans within the city and form groups. They wanted to be among those that were immune to Z's. If they are bitten by a Z, that bite will instantly kill the Z. The same people who had this natural defense were also the ones that when a Zombie encountered that person, it did not even acknowledge them. Those were the only people that the occupants could hope to be around and survive.

Even though they could not help, the cities were still being watched and monitored by those in Teton and other locations scattered throughout the world. These were the places where groups of humans, scientists, doctors, and others were researching cures for humans. The labs would run all day long with experimentations rolling one after another to find ways to destroy the Zombies and Z. These were the last of mankind's Science, Medical, and Technology human survivors.

All the remaining groups agreed to monitor the events as they happened that the cities were indeed running out of humans. The big question for them to brainstorm as of late has been, what would happen to the Zombies and Z without any food source? Would they die of starvation or what?

For the forgotten, those that were on a mission and were left behind had long ago run out of ammunition. Their only weapons were knives, swords, spears, baseball bats, to name a few; typical melee stuff. These would require direct contact with the creature, unlike a bullet.

Direct contact with a Z could kill them, as long as a sword, spear, or some sharp object is driven into the heart of a Z. Another way of getting them was getting them in the brain. Crushing the brain, head or cutting it off worked in killing both the creatures, though piercing the heart did not work for Zombies. The Zombies did not have a beating heart like humans; the Z's did.

The Sheep had been too coward in the past to attack, though, which was why more of them had been dying. But being grouped up with other Sheep or Sheep in Wolves Clothes that had adapted changed their attitudes. They started giving names to the Zombie slayers and those who died. Victors were those that encountered a Z or Zombie and slain either of them in an encounter. Victims were those that ended up dead and became a Zombie meal.

The forgotten ones were roving about the city with their melee weapons, carrying out scouting missions for food and supplies, killing all Zs and Zombies in their path. They called these Nest Missions, which aimed to seek during the daytime the resting Zombies. These were the creatures avoiding the sun. Those missions were to clean out killing all Zombies and Z's in densely Z populated areas, who guarded the Zombies during the day time.

Once these began, the Zombies were quick to adapt and seek out new locations. The previous areas had been where the Z and Zombies were typically at the center of these large cities. The Zombies began to go away from those former locations as a survival tactic to find new shelters and to sweep new cities to seek food.

Since the humans were becoming extinct in every major city, The Zs were eating all other meat they could find, even if it was rotten, and saving the humans for Zombies. The harmony continued in this way.

Each night the Zombies and Z's would continue to move in groups of their own, moving towards the outskirts of each of the cities which were still being monitored. Those watching knew well that the satellites and drones would soon need to be replaced from vacant cities to the ones where Z's and Zombies were migrating. What good will the older cameras do there since barely anyone was left alive in those previously highly populated cities?

Especially the cities that were smaller in square miles were becoming empty. Humans, Z's, and Zombies were all gone, either dead or traveling. As for the larger cities such as New York, Los Angeles, Chicago, Houston, to name a few, the scientists predicted it could take a month or so before all the Z's and Zombies may empty those cities too. After that, the predictions claimed they would attack the rural locations, which lacked the technology and housed the purest Wolves.

With more groups of Zombies and Z than satellites, choices had to be made about which group will be followed.

The scientists began assigning names to the groups of Zombies to continue the monitoring uninterrupted. This would take several scientists put on 3-6 hour shifts.

It was only a matter of time when all the former major cities transformed into ghost towns. Once the Teton groups were assured of it, the missions began again, but this time it was different. They had to target secure, important, and viable locations. Once at these locations, they had to ensure it was both Z and Zombie-free. Z and Zombies that were returning were kept an eye for and conveniently killed.

Once these locations became completely eradicated of any Z or Zombie threats, barriers were put in place, along with security. These became new human-made shelters, like mini-safe zones. These sanctuaries were to have specific regulations, and work was going to be easier. The humans now had the chance to complete and safely progress forward in ways that have not been seen since the year 2019.

Each of the cities which have been chosen for these shelters were places that had significant and important resources. These were needed to ensure the survival of man. Hope began to spark for an era free from the Zombie Virus. People were starting to dream again.

In North America, 20 major cities were chosen as the most important ones and for the following resources:

#20 Pittsburgh <Steel and metal Production>

#19 Baltimore <Industrial Minerals, Fuel Resources>

#18 San Diego <Fishing, Produce, Natural Resources>

#17 Denver <Resources, Technology>

#16 San Jose <Technology, Medical>

#15 Detroit <Manufacturing, Medical>

#14 Phoenix <Natural Resources, Minerals, Technology>

#13 Seattle <Technology, Minerals, Produce>

#12 Miami <Produce, Fishing, Medical, Science, Technology>

#11 Atlanta <Produce, Technology, Medical, Minerals>

#10 Boston <Technology, Medical, Science>

#09 Philadelphia <Medical, Technology, Science>

#08 San Francisco <Medical, Technology, Fishing>

#07 Dallas <Natural Resources, Produce, LIfe stock, Technology, Minerals, Medical>

#06 Houston <Natural Resources, Life Stock, Produce, Minerals, Medical Technology, Fuel>

#05 Washington <Technology, Weapons, Medical>

#04 Chicago <Manufacturing, Fishing, Medical>

#03 Los Angeles <Technology, Produce, Natural Resources, Medical, Science, Fuel>

#02 New York <Medical, Science, Technology, Manufacturing>

#01 Teton, Wyoming: Home Base locations of all operations to save Mankind from Extinction.

The only city that was already secure was Teton. It was on the list for being the base of operations. No damage could come to this city. It must be secure from all threats, whether from Z, Zombie, or anything else <nature, man or animal>. The remaining were prioritized as important locations with their promising surroundings.

As for the cities outside of the 20, they were under the control of either Zombies or some smaller communities living the nomadic life. These were either those who were traveling and were on the road or those that were remaining tribes of Wolves who lived in rural areas, away from the large cities.

The towns near the major cities were going to have their first encounter with the Z and Zombies. Most of them had no idea what was heading towards them night by night – which were armies of Z creatures. Some of these towns included those who had previously left the city yet only covered a short distance. They had planned to stay nearby to make supply runs when it was needed.

All of the 20 cities had food banks, and those food banks had warehouses. If not all, most of them had enough food to feed up to 15 million people for three months. One such land was Los Angeles. Cities, where the 1% may have once lived, were rich in medical supplies, technology, and possibly even weapons and ammunition. Some of the 1%, when they did fall to the Z and Zombies, kept their stored resources safe.

When that 1% went back for those hidden treasures, they usually found what they had stored. Others found more than they had expected, while some found nothing but destruction. The latter's homes turned out to be plundered, leaving behind only things that did not matter in this new world, including truckloads of cash. In this new world, what was important was weapons, guns, rifles, bullets, explosives, swords, bow and arrows, medicine, drugs, liquor, food, shelter.

The news began to spread then. The only direction man could take to recover from the virus was based on getting the 20 cities up and running. They were designed as a fort against the Z or Zombie attack, for the rescuers and rescued, Sheep and Wolves to coexist alike. These cities laid special emphasis on reproduction and reproductive facilities to allow man to populate the world again.

Within a month, barriers were put up in the most important locations, in 18 of the 20 cities. New York and Los Angeles had yet to be barricaded. The difficulty with that was that both of these cities had quite a few critical areas that needed secure barriers to begin outermost protection. Phase 2 was to begin re-population and to orient skilled workers for essential services to go fully operational. Rules of the city were also to be laid down for order to prevail.

The Scientists had one of their conferences in Teton where the Chief of Operations, Riley O Neele, announced, "The birth rate of mankind has continued to decline everywhere, with the exception of Wolves-dominated areas in the rural areas and small towns. Their numbers of new births have stayed about the same, if not increased in rates since the year 2020. The biggest concern pertaining to those that belong to the Sheep is they are without medical care. Most of the births among them have been mysteriously unsuccessful. More than 50% of the newborns were dead at the time of birth, killing off both Mother and Baby. Would Mr. Stanley like to take charge and speak on that?"

A weary old Stoic scientist stood up and said, "As for the mothers that have survived have been those that gave birth to the children. Despite that, reports claim that a large percentage of those children died within the first five days or less. We have not been able to pinpoint the cause, but no medicine or medical assistance has proved to be resolutely successful. It is hence part of our project to investigate what the Wolves are doing differently to procreate, we do have some theories, now we require conclusions."

O Neele takes over again. "The cities we are creating are going to be viable. Hospitals would be needed; people would need to fall in love. That's the environment we need to reform. With most of the world's population at the lowest numbers since the age of modern man, we can do nothing but persevere for the sake of our forefathers. The 20 cities we are planning with the help of some esteemed Urban developers will be able to provide enough space, resources, and viable items that man will require to not only survive but live. And that is why these 20 cities have been chosen."

A round of applause erupted, reverberating all about the base. With that, phase 2 of the operations was announced to proceed at full speed. Planes and helicopters began working non-stop. Every trip going out of Teton also went to one of the other 19 cities and even areas such as the remaining Safe Zones.

The trips entering into one of the 20 cities brought passengers, comprising all essential workers to restore the cities and make it a place for humans to call home and be safe and secure. The planes or helicopters that leave to Teton or one of the Safe Zones always returned stocked with supplies. These were promised to be distributed to help with the battle, which soon emerged between the Zs and Zombies versus Man.

Chapter 14
The Agreement

For the first time since 2022, guns, rifles, ammunition, and armory had started to be manufactured. Cities came to a consensus; Detroit was to make handguns and rifles in mass quantity, Washington D.C. to make bulletproof vests and helmets, and Chicago was to manufacture the bullets for both the rifles and handguns. Three different locations for each item were deliberated to maintain a safety protocol and prevent another rebellion between Humans, unlike the Safe Zones tragedy. These cities were chosen because they had machines to mass produce, which could be altered for the tasks at hand. They were also near Pittsburgh, the Steel City, with the major steel mills that provided the raw material for the manufacture of handguns and rifles and the shells for the bullets.

The manufacturing took ten days to begin at full force. The workers worked in shifts of 12 hours per day, six days a week, allowing the manufacturing to be non-stop, to prepare for the Zombies and Z's.

The other cities: Baltimore, San Jose, Denver, San Diego, Phoenix, Seattle, Miami, Atlanta, Boston, Philadelphia, San Francisco, Dallas, and Houston, also were on track in a few days. These places required more time to secure due to the industries and vicinities of these industries with leftover Zombies and Z's looming around. Their barriers also took longer to construct, but men and women were at it hard. Once they were done, the event of a Zombie or Z attacking or attempting to return to these cities became minimum.

New York and Los Angeles required more time to clear and secure than any other city. They had areas that had yet to be blocked off, had barriers to secure and ensure that no Zombie or Z could gain access. Until New York and Los Angeles were completely cleared and verified, no human workers (only Zombie and Z-slayers) were transported to these two cities.

The rapid developments that were happening around these lands, though, did not start on a whim. It had all begun with an agreement.

***

Back in Teton, Gus was hailed as the man who recruited members from the purest Wolves clans. He had been the leader on the missions to villages and small towns, the first to respond to the Red and Yellow X's signals. Every group Gus had encountered accepted to send members of their community to Teton; some sent as few as five members, some as many as nine members. Even though they all lived many miles away from each other, their values were the same and adapted to become the same as they learned about the new world order.

At Teton, they learned more of what was happening to the USA and the Entire World. They had initially back at home been slightly concerned that the knowledge might have all been a trick by the government to get their firearms and weapons. Yet, it wasn't a trick. What they had been told was proven true at Teton.

A few days after all the Wolves had been gathered and they all formed camaraderie, Gus invited all of them. Before that, the Wolves from the different parts of the country at Teton had spent time together carrying out private discussions between themselves. No member was from or a part of Teton. In that meeting, Gus gave them terms to agree with for the new human world setup. Those Wolves may have been Country People, but they were not by any means, dumb or stupid. They were simply Americans who loved the glorious nation that the USA had erstwhile been. And so they had first come to terms, willing to fight against the governments and the 1% who controlled those government officials. It did concern them that Teton had more surviving 1% than any other location in the world, though it had astounded them that the majority of 1% were no more.

From among the discussions they had carried out, they speculated that someone had to be in charge and decide. Which must have included, they thought, the decision to come to agreements. They had other matters of concern and questions too that demanded answers.

"The first concern we have is who's in charge of Teton? Is it one person or a few people? Who will be calling the shots and running the operations after the agreement? Those that will give orders, will those orders be expected compliance without any questions? Or is it going to be democratic as we Wolves do, bringing issues and concerns to all, and then everyone has a vote in the matter the majority vote forms an agreement?"

Another member rose in the meeting called by Gus. It was a young boy who was one of the most skillful warriors. "The second concern we have is a follow-up. If an agreement is made, how will the leader be chosen? If there is a group, who will determine who will be in that group of decision-makers?" It was a woman's turn this time.

She said, "The third concern we have is about the guns and weapons that we Wolves have got in our tribes currently. Will y'all expect the Wolves to hand over the rifles, guns, ammunition, and weapons that we have stockpiled? Even to this day, we continue to make bullets to stockpile. If y'all Teton people expect or even demand that all weapons be given to them freely, that would be a huge mistake. Just saying."

While the Teton people looked at each other, thinking of their replies, the first Wolf started again, "At this point, we do not need Teton, rather Teton needs us. All of us before you have been doing fine without any outside help. We don't have any reported cases or even any Zombies or Z's sightings; all those in attendance can confirm that for you. We owe you for informing us and hosting us, and that is where your favor to us ends. Half of us had repaid by hosting you, if you want to look at it that way, but well.

"The community of the Wolves was the first to denounce our faith in governments. We especially knew that the 1% didn't care for anyone but themselves. We found the way of life that was most fulfilling, and it showed, for the wrath of Zombies and Z's came to strike you, not us. All that is important to us visitors is if we give our hand in support, how will disagreements and resource distribution be handled?

After a few minutes, Gus spoke up. "Among us have been some of the more sensitive members from the group of 1%. We've carried out numerous rescue missions and exterminated many Zombies and Z's from areas where Sheep and City Wolves both resided. It is true that we have been in control and have been used to being final decision-makers, normally."

He paused and looked at the members surrounding him. "I'll admit it's true. Time has changed, and too much is at stake, and both our sides are aware of that. All mankind has to unite and work for the same goal together now. The survival of humans and the future for all dangles still. Even the 1% among us know this, and so do you and everyone else aware of the Vid-26.

"We at Teton need the Wolves. You all know the reasons, the Wolves are better equipped and had been training for a war against anyone wanting to threaten their lifestyle, their freedoms, and especially their guns and weapons. I am the leader of the rescue missions who has spent more time with the Wolves than any other person from Teton, and I will completely empathize with you."

The Teton people knew that if an agreement was not made, the Wolves would return home and let those of Teton figure what to do by themselves in Teton. Teton was aware that the Sheep's former occupants couldn't be trusted with weapons, that the Sheep were not trained with firearms such as all the Wolves were.

Opposed to that, even the youngest of Wolves could hold a handgun. It was like a Sparta against a middle-aged adult that was a Sheep or a 1%. The oldest of Wolves had little to no fear of death and would be more than happy to kill Zombies and Z's as long as they could pull a trigger; Gus knew that.

But Gus and his team were also aware that Teton had things that could help the Wolves fight. Teton had advanced technology: they could control satellites to watch and monitor the activity of Zombies and Z. They had satellite telephones, advanced weapons such as rocket launchers, explosives, drones, and other technology to aid for any battles or encounters with the Zombies and Z.

Teton also had world-class doctors in every field of medicine, state of the art medical equipment, and medical supplies for any injuries or illnesses that could and did happen. Most of the groups did have doctors for the Wolves, yet they were limited in equipment, medicine, and specialization such as against cancer, heart disease, etc.

Teton also had equipment such as planes, helicopters, cargo planes to transfer tanks, vehicles, supplies, people, food, raw materials, minerals, fuel, and other viable and important items, which the Wolves didn't have. They could restock these items when needed or required. After all, when the human population declined as fast as it did, these supplies were in storage warehouses, military bases, and government centers that could feed all remaining humans for 20 or more years. Supplies were still abundant in the world, only getting to them and transporting them back was the problem; for the Wolves, not for Teton.

The Wolves became aware of the advantages that those from Teton offered, yet the one thing that Teton couldn't provide was additional battle-ready humans.

They proclaimed it after a week's worth of back-and-forths that Wolves were the people that needed to be leading the attacks and counter-attacks against the Zombies and Z. This had been after the Wolves threatened, "If you're not willing to negotiate and ensure what we agree on will actually happen, then we will ask to be returned back home. That way you can do what you want without our help and assistance."

Gus knew that the Wolves were not bluffing. They also knew that the reasoning behind making the Wolves lead in the attack was the smartest. His 1% background was nothing in this new world, for money was just paper. It was as good to be used as toilet paper, to start campfires. Those who still had money saved were just as wealthy and equal as those who didn't have any money.

Gus made use of his strong points and convinced those in Teton that it would be best to agree to terms and to work with the Wolves to make the team of Wolves and those of Teton and the other safe zones to work together against the Zombies and Z. It was the best chance for all mankind to survive and have a future.

A mutual decision had to be worked out. It was agreed that 11 members would vote on issues. Four of the 11 would be Teton people. The remaining seven would be those chosen by the Wolves. Teton finalized this arrangement to show good faith and ensured that the Wolves had the majority of votes by nearly a two to one margin.

Gus, the leader of those from Teton, was one of the four representatives from Teton. The remaining seven members were decided by the Wolves, by vote. This group of men and women agreed on several things mutually with the people of Teton. That sealed the deal for the agreement to be done, and all were in agreement.

The first agreement was that all issues brought and discussed would be voted on by the 11 people. The majority vote will determine the decision. The Wolves were a majority in numbers, yet the chosen Wolves were intent on making the decision they believed was best for all humans. Gus was confident that there was relative diversity within the Wolves themselves and the chosen ones were intelligent people. He had chosen the best from amongst himself, whom he could tell had selflessness traits in them. These people knew that being rich did not matter over here. Only lives did, as well as the survival of mankind.

All that the Wolves initially requested was on keeping their guns and not handing them over to Teton. This decision had all seven votes from the Wolves and also Gus's vote from Teton. Gus was true to his word of making the best decisions keeping all of humanity in mind. The weaponry of the Wolves could make the Teton people greedy.

The good faith also meant that the Wolves would agree with the decisions of those that were from Teton. A sense of mutual respect and appropriate harmony was developed between the voting parties. No one person was in charge that had more authority than the others in the group of 11. Every member had an equal voice and just one vote in all matters.

It was this group of 11 who decided what cities to save. The list of 19 cities that were deemed necessary emerged from their decision-making. These 19 cities promised safe rehabilitation of humans to ensure that supplies and weapons would continue in their production and stockpiling. The war could take years or decades to rid the world of Z and Zombies eventually. That's what they kept in mind when preparing.

The 19 cities were agreed upon, after which the next agreement was to reach out to other locations throughout North America to find more groups of Wolves as well as humans that had not been discovered.

It was agreed by the 11 that to integrate those who lived in small towns and cities in their army to fight the Zombies and Z's, they had to bring more representatives together, either to Teton or to one of the nearby Safe Zones. As soon as any of the 19 cities was secured, the Wolves and others could be taken to those areas. It would depend on the proximity of the discovered people as to where they would be placed.

The newly discovered groups were met with a team comprising Teton people and the Wolves from Teton. These Wolves were better suited to understand what their community members were learning about the status quo for the first time, including the build-up to Vid-26, the Zombie Virus, and the emergence of Zombies and Z's.

Some Wolves discovered during these missions had lived nearby the former great cities that had encountered Zombies and Z's. Hence they had some idea about the world's state if not only about Zombies and Z's. For instance, they had discovered that the Zombies and Z's could be killed by piercing a bullet in their head or heart. But their knowledge was consummated by the Teton recruitment group. They learned this was happening all over the world.

Many of these Wolves agreed to join at higher percentages than older groups. They varied in sizes; sometimes, there would be as few as 20 Wolves in some small towns. In others, there could be several thousand Wolves. All of them had to go through orientation given by usually the Wolves at Teton.

The threat of the Vid-26, the Zombies, and Z made the groups of Wolves realize that out there, traveling every night in the darkness searching for humans, were Zombies. They could secretly strike them, and some towns were indeed small to have succumbed to their attacks. Even Wolves needed a pack to fight against a greater, stronger threat that had them outnumbered by huge margins.

The Wolves agreed to join when they learned that the 1% and government had fallen and were no more. They then heard how the decisions were to be made through a majority vote by a group that included mostly Wolves. Upon that, learning that these newly discovered Wolves would keep their weapons and guns now encouraged them all the more to join the Teton recruitment group.

The only request by those that had just been discovered was that if they were to be moved to help against the Zombies and Z, the entire group had to stay together and not be separated. They said, "Even if one of our women gets pregnant, her fighting group had to stay with her. They cannot be transferred to a location where they were battling the Zombies and Z's or any other high-risk areas or any other area without the pregnant woman. This was common with the Wolves that agreed to join and help.

The counterstrike and humans working together against the Zombies and Z were now even larger than before. It was the first time since COVID19 that all humans were working together regardless of their associations. They were working for one cause to keep man from going extinct. More Wolves were joining every hour as soon as they became aware of what was at stake.

Many of the Wolves discovered were saved with the agreement in place. Their towns had been where the Zombies and Z's had been roving. Those locations would have put certain communities of Wolves at risk. Had the agreement not been made, countless Wolves would have been killed in a matter of days or weeks against the Zombies and Z's that were headed in their direction. They had left the city from where they were created and were out searching for humans in newer lands, especially with the wildlife, where the Z could survive. Near to the jungles and woods were where many of the Wolves had made their rural homes.

Time was nearing when not only will the undiscovered Wolves in rural areas be under the attack of Zombies and Z's, but also those that were at 158 of remaining Safe Zones. With Teton's attention laid onto the Wolves, could they have predicted how gravely in danger the Safe Zones were?

Chapter 15
The 158

With the ongoing development of the 19 essential cities, New York, Los Angeles, Chicago, Washington D.C., and Houston, to name a few, the remaining 158 operating Safe Zones had been busy working 24 hours a day non-stop. They were working to help the very 19 cities.

Each of these safe zones had their horde of warriors fighting and protecting the Safe Zones from approaching Zombies or Z's. These warriors that have survived the longest had a background in some form of military. They had experienced fighting soldiers across borders and having bullets flying in their direction, trying to kill them. These men and women were happy to serve the people in these battles. Particularly, there was no guilt involved nor that nationality crap. The Zombies and Z's were dangerous only as long as they were close-range. They were never allowed to come close-ranged.

Most of these skilled warriors had been transferred to the cities during the initial stages and designated to help clear the location making sure it is Zombie- and Z-free. They took care of nearby fields, woods, buildings, etc. After that, they would be posted as guards, and other members would set up cameras with motion sensors.

The next step was to double-check the place and see if it was still free of all creatures. If yes, then a portion of that group would begin to create barriers to either stop or at least slow down the Zombies or Zs if they found the cities. They were predicted to return from the wild if they did, that's where most of them would be last seen.

Securing the locations, creating barriers to keep those secured areas safe, preparing for humans to return, and opening up necessary industries to give a man a fighting chance to survive. This was the set of instructions that were carried out in steps.

A mix of both Sheep and those non-Sheep members who returned filled all the industrial positions to get things working and reach the end goal. These occupants and the cities did not have guns or weapons with them. It had seemed that the Revolt of the 7 former Safe Zones was never going to be forgotten.

Those that had been saved from the nearby city, who were running the missions, were sent to the places with the most beneficial extracts and scouting for the needs of all mankind. The few families that had remained were belonging to Sheep; they were allowed to stay together. Among the husbands and wives, where both were essential workers, the one who was skilled in areas identified as most important would be the family's location.

As for the other Sheep, those who didn't have essential skills remained at the location. Either that or they would be transferred to places that needed manual labor help. Many of them would end up working on farms, picking fruit and vegetables. Some would work on cattle ranches as a rancher. Others would find a position within one of the operating or future manufacturing places that required manual help.

Neither of their jobs would allow them to possess a gun or firearm. Even for those few Sheep that were once military or law enforcement agents, and especially for those individuals that were trained with deadly weapons. A few Sheep did remain at the 158 free zones. Some had proven their loyalty and were still warriors. Others were either cooks or worked maintenance. All who were allowed to remain behind had been those that never caused trouble.

They did what was asked of them, which was the only way to earn your place at a Safe Zone. It was, in fact, these Safe Zones that were better run and maintained with the few but good Sheep.

The word was being spread from Free Zone to Free Zone that the Zombie and Z attacks were increasing, and nearly half of the 158 remaining free zones would need reinforcements soon. Some of the groups of Z's and Zombies were marching in the thousands, possibly even tens of thousands. Some free zones got attacked out of the blue at night, falling and being left with no survivors, for the numbers of the Z and Zombie were just so great. They were only being added on with more extinctions of Free Zones.

The reinforcements took their time. Meanwhile, the Free Zones were being attacked by a few hundred or lesser Zombies and Z's at night. These Safe Zone locations were alert though and prevented getting overrun and overtaken by the Zombies and Z's. The humans were victorious in these locations. Teton had been aware of what was happening. Finally, their preparations were completed, and it was agreed by all 11 decision-makers that help must be sent to all locations except where they were aware no humans survived.

Even if just one human were alive, a small team would be sent to recover and transport the living. For the Free Zones that were attacked and had 65% or greater survival rate, greater teams would be sent to reinforce and prepare for the next round of Zombie and Z attacks once the sunset.

The community of Wolves that belonged to the 11 and others had reached out to more Wolves in the still-functioning Free Zones for help. Some traveled by 4-wheel drive; others would arrive by motorcycles. Some even landed on horses.

As the Wolves started to arrive, those that had just battled all night thought to themselves, "Is this it, is this all the help we will receive?" But as time passed, more and more Wolves and survivors of some of the Free Zones arrived.

With nearly an hour till the Sun to set, helicopters started arriving. Ropes came down, and additional reinforcements dropped. Those from the Free Zone were expecting to see more men and women with the same uniforms as they wore.

But the dropped ones were not wearing any uniform. These were Wolves who wore their traditional simple hunting attires. That's what made them distinct.

As the night arrived, the first of the Z's began to attack. The Wolves outshined all the rest, proving they had been practiced in firearms their entire lives. These Sheep and City Wolves were left jaw-dropped by the number of creatures a single Wolf was consuming. It simultaneously inspired some, while others felt their contributions might not even be needed.

In many Safe Zones, when the Sun was out, traps and obstacles would be put in place by the Wolves, who trained others. They had been hunters their entire life and knew exactly how to hunt species that traveled in large numbers. These snares proved effective as well. Some sleeping Zombies would be in hiding and would counterattack with some success. But the Wolves would usually attack more potently.

Some of the Z and Zombie groups were approaching by the thousands. They were laid to waste most of the humans that had set up their zones, camps, and societies along the way.

Those who survived in these Zones or communities knew that the previous night's danger would only be even greater the next night. These were communicated by members of the Wolves with Teton's help and trained to set up traps on their phones to ambush the groups of Z's and Zombies during the daylight.

Having traps set up served two purposes. First, it would have the Zombies and Z's battling away from the Free Zone territory/camps, significantly reducing their numbers. Secondly, the Zombies and Z's could be distracted to a different location where the human population had a better chance to win, away from those vulnerable Safe Zones. This would also allow additional time for members of these new Safe Zones to prepare for the Zombies and Z's as they neared their area.

These Free Zones were also receiving Wolf reinforcements for preparation. The Teton groups had to ensure the survival of maximum humans. However, not all Free Zones survived. Some, even with the Wolves and reinforcements' aid, lost their lives. They had not expected the abilities of larger hordes of Z's and Zombies, which just crippled them.

There were free zone areas dotted near the former highly-populated cities such as New York, Los Angeles, Chicago, Houston, etc. While these cities were safe from major attacks, the free zones nearby were scrambling and falling apart. Battalions of Z and Zombie populations infested them, seeking food.

Countless lives were lost on the few nights these free zone locations were invaded along with others. The only silver lining was that none of the cities were being attacked. Even though the troops would try to prepare themselves to be ready, there were no signs of any Zombie or Z. Unfortunately for the newly barricaded cities, their Free Zone outposts were destroyed with the attacks, setting them and their planned operations back.

Surveillance was mostly happening from inside. Drones and satellites would be useful for keeping a watchful eye, but that was the extent of it. Delays would set in since human force needed to be established to keep guard on the free zones that were no longer available. Security was recuperated and tightened to hold off any further Zombie or Z attacks.

The people in these lands were doing twice as much during the day and then further had to be prepared for battle at night at all the major free zones. The few that had yet to be attacked predicted upcoming attacks in the nights to come. Those free zones were still in operation and reinforced at the constant within the three days since the first reported attacks in major free zones.

Some zones were eating up smaller groups of Zombies and Z attacking. They and those in Teton were the only locations that were safe as the third night began. Geared up and ready for battle, the trembling soldiers could feel this night was going to be different. Their supplies and reinforcements were far greater than before. Traps had been set, explosives and landmines all were in place. Security was also increased, and those of the Free Zones had many Wolves fighting side by side. It seemed like the ultimate showdown, but they knew a lot more was to come.

All eyes were set on the dimming sun. It disappeared, and soon enough, the first of the Z could be seen arriving from the curve of the horizon. It was part of Wolves' plan to leave the security barrier of the rebuilt free zone compounds and bring to the fight half a mile or so from there.

Soon enough, a deadly battle broke out in the open land. It extended across two nights, at the end of which thousands of Zombies and Z's were wiped out and were trailing. The Wolves, bloody and unbowed, chased behind them, following them surreptitiously. They had to learn where the creatures were going during the daytime when the sun was out. Over their heads, drones also flew.

No sooner, the humans had locations for a surprise counter-attack. Zombies and Z's hid in the narrow pathways on the way towards minor free zones. Human forces discussed amongst themselves and found that explosives would be most efficient to exterminate the creatures. For the Wolves, it was like shooting fish in a barrel – they did so maniacally. That marked the conclusion for a huge Zombie and Z army.

Some more free zones put out spies that could locate the Z's protecting the Zombies in caves and caverns that kept out the sunlight. The Wolves and Warriors intended to kill off all the Z's that were protecting the sleeping Zombies. Here, they had a couple of thoughts about how the idea of using explosives could work.

The first one was that a large explosive blast could seal the cave, and they could only hope there wasn't a way to leave that cave via another exit. Alternatively, if the cave couldn't be sealed, it could make a huge enough blast to create an opening that would allow sunlight to pour into the cave. The deadly sun rays would kill off the sleeping, resting Zombies.

Sure enough, the latter happened. The first blast caused the roof to fall, and the cavern was exposed to the light of day. Zombies shrieked as if they were burning in hellfire. Wolves enjoyed the sights as they fell dying while being trapped. Meanwhile, other trackers seized the chance to kill as many Zombies and Z's that were within gunfire distance while they protected themselves under the sunlight.

Trackers started looking out for additional trails leading to other caves and secluded dark places. Some humans from a few free zones couldn't ambush them here, for the day was ending, and they knew they needed to be better armed for any counter-attacks against the Zombies. Regardless, it was a day to celebrate for the Wolves and Sheep all. They looked ahead to preparing for attacks on the following night.

Some backs and forths followed until the end of the 5th night since the first attacks. Only 64 free zones remained in operation. The rest either had their barriers broken or breached by the Zs and Zombies. In some other locations, forces of Zombies and Z's had been annihilated by the united forces of mankind.

In these battles, technology and brainpower played a huge role in reaping success. Each failure allowed humans an opportunity to improve with the next attack. They could communicate with Teton, the operations base, and other free zones to be in perfect sync. When strategies worked out effectively, that was shared with the others.

The tactics that failed were also shared by those that remained in the free zones. Those ideas would either be disposed to be used again or built upon better.

More forces started to be sent out during the daytime to look for Zombies in caves, caverns, or enclosed dark spaces. These locations were scouted and either destroyed or sunlight was expose upon the Zombies in hiding.

The other locations that had any human survivors were also being located during the day, with rescue teams being sent there. Some of the survivors would be found bitten. While there would be scarce hope for some, and they would have to be killed before their transformation, a percentage of those that were bitten had the natural defense that immediately would kill the Z that bit them.

As these attacks went on, the plans for re-opening those 19 essential cities were put on hold. All those at the cities and those who survived the attacks on the Free Zones were being picked up and returned to Teton. That's where they were determining the next action to take. Both forces of creatures and humans had faced considerable losses. There had been defeats as well as victories in the last five days. It was decided that even at the locations in the US where man was successful against the Zombies and Z, all humans would need to regroup and return to Teton to gather together and prepare to eliminate all Zombies and Z's once and for all.

The Free Zones started getting wrapped up for the foreseeable future. This meant all the 19 essential cities had to cease all operations and return to Teton as well. The Zombies had given humans tough competition in all major battles; this war was far from over.

The elected leaders of Teton knew that these battles could not be won by manpower alone. A lot of humans dying were resuscitating as Zombies. So unless the scientists could create an effective weapon such as artificial sunlight or weapons that had the special survival gene that will help survive against both Zombie and Z bites, chances appeared slim.

Some injection guns based on the latter concept were prototyped. While these developed weapons could kill the Z instantly when used, it didn't work against the Zombies based on the found gene amongst humans wasn't effective against the Zombies but only against the Z.

The only humans that had hopes for manpower fights were the Wolves. They were up to the task and had been far more effective than the Sheep in the last few battles. Even though they were leading from the front, it was for every 70 Sheep that one Wolf had been dying. And the Sheep had been dying a lot.

All of the remaining mankind finally made it to Teton. Teton became the only place that was secured entirely 75 miles in all directions. Land mines were in place, fencing and barriers had been modified. It was made certain that every mile that the Zombies and Z's would have to travel to reach Teton would become more difficult for them than the previous due to the intensity of the obstacles in place.

Areas that were close by and known to have places where the Zombies could hide during the day were being destroyed now through aircraft mostly, which had been limited in numbers. Only areas near Teton were being targeted for these attacks. It became nearly impossible for the Zombies to reach Teton. Without places to rest during the daytime, the sun was out, crippling the Zs and Zombies from making it to Teton. Several had also been dying, roving through the night, unable to find shelter for morning and sometimes even food.

Chapter 16
The Science

The scientists in Teton worked day and night for solutions against the creatures. They were developing both weapons based on special human genes. They named the chromosome Z as the natural gene, which was highly effective against the Z's. Chromosome Z meant instant death for the Z. However, the problem persisted that the Zombies wouldn't die from chromosome Z.

Instead, the experiments revealed that the Zombies were getting groggy and leaving one with the chromosome Z alone. Other Zombies would somehow know in advance if that human was previously bitten. These humans were as if they were invisible to the Zombies. In this way, the Z chromosome acted as a natural repellant against these creatures.

Other scientists still alive and working worldwide had started creating more powerful artificial light rays that would defend against Zombie attacks. Israel and France were pioneering countries here. Other nations further modified these to be used as a weapon during battles with the Zombies. These light rays were not effective against the Z, though. The Z had natural protection in the sunlight. It proved deadly only against the Zombies.

Simultaneously, other weapons were also being developed based on chromosome Z. Teton was mass-producing this miraculous gene to be used against the Z. Some of the weapons designed were bullets that had been dipped in the Z chromosome. Once this bullet hit a Z in any location, the Z was found to die from it instantly. This weapon was revolutionary since, in the previous battles, many Sheep's lives were lost since they could not aim the head or the creatures' hearts.

Aerosol sprays with chromosome Z had also been created to attack the Z through exposure to their skin and the exposed air with the Z Chromosome spray. All these weapons were being tested at the Teton location on the live Zombies and Z's.

"Artificial lighting against the Zombies could be used during even the darkest of night. Weapons with Chromosome Z are highly effective against the Z. This is a revolutionary time since the Zombie Virus and could be hailed as the turning point in the books of history." The lead scientist announced this in the mass address at Teton.

"We are still at work trying to develop more ways to utilize this knowledge and find ways to improve both security and offense. Whatever means there are out there that could be discovered to erase Zombies and Z's off the face of the earth would be employed. The human population is estimated to be at an all-time low. No one had the right figures, but we all remain in some hundreds of thousands. We cannot become extinct, and so the creatures will have to go."

A rallying cry of the crowds followed the address.

Testing continued on further discoveries. It was soon realized that since the aerosol spray was harmless against humans, it could be applied to the skin. As soon as this was confirmed, those that were to go on missions in areas with Z's or Zombies would be sprayed down twice.

One would be before leaving Teton and the second time once they arrived at their destination. The aerosol spray was being applied to every member on those missions. In addition to the spray being used to work against the Z, all weapons from guns to rifles and even arrowheads for arrows had been modified to employ the chromosome Z and artificial lights. This meant both Z's and Zombies were in danger since these hybrid weapons could kill both using lighting and chromosome attachments. Even swords, spears, knives, all the melee weapons were being modified with one or both of these inventions.

Helicopters, planes, and even lighting systems at Teton and on missions started employing these weapons. The lights were added to ensure protection from possible Zombie attacks in the form of streetlights and were used for hunting and killing Zombies through flashlights during the nighttime on missions. The latter opportunity allowed the scouting for supplies easier for humans, adding on the layers of protection and around Teton.

After a long time, humans again had a reason to be hopeful. There was a fighting chance to not only survive but to put an end to this event, the Zombie Virus. Once enough weapons were manufactured, it was only a matter of time when the operations to retake the 20 essential cities would continue from where it had left off. Humans could taste that victorious era of rebuilding.

Some teams in the 19 cities were being sent already, fully equipped. All the former initial steps were put in place again. It started with inspections and ensured that the Zombies and Z's had not occupied these cities since the evacuation. The nearby areas were being inspected around the cities to ensure that repopulating would continue without worrying about Zombies and Z's.

The next step, unlike last time, was to secure the areas with large artificial lighting systems. These were mounted on large poles in optimal locations as a defense as soon as the darkness would fall. Once set up after tireless endeavors, this simple change allowed mankind the chance to sleep better at night after the hard work during the day.

After these measures, humans were again being transported to the 19 essential cities. The rebuild process began, and it was made sure that enough lighting and Z chromosome could also be manufactured in the cities than only in Teton to give all surviving humans a chance to win the Zombie Virus War.

In 2027, after eight years, man was once again the aggressor, not just the defender, mostly once the cities were up and running. Mass productions of both historic weapons had begun with the industrial setups in place. Many taskforces of Sheep had been trained in manufacturing back in Teton, so the people knew what they had to do. They were now producing these non-stop, 24 hours a day, with rotating shifts of workers.

A few weeks ago, these weapons had been a fantasy, but mankind had once again prevailed. Humanity was proud of itself, especially for the lighting since the Zombies were much harder to kill than the Z. Teton and the 19 cities had been the first to be fully installed and secured with these lights, allowing man to again repopulate those great cities that once saw human civilization occupy spaces freely long before the COVID-19 and the COVID-26. All the incentive and subsidy that people needed to fight and manufacture was the hope for ending this war and living in peace.

The cities began to light up at night. Humans that were either stranded or traveling on the road or stationed in rural areas that were yet to be found started seeing these lights that radiated like the Sun night. Many of those that spotted these lights cautiously approached these places where they would instantly be welcomed and offered a chance to be a part of that society after being briefed and oriented. They would be given a chance to help with any task or training they desired.

The Zombies and Z's also saw these lights. The former would die instantly, while for the latter, the night-guards at their post would suffice.

Life and operations in these 19 cities were being restored. On one of the scouting missions, a team discovered a few former military bases. At these former military bases, weapons were also located. These were sent back to be modified for lighting attachments and chromosome Z bullets.

The warriors going out on missions, sprayed down twice with the chromosome Z, became invisible to the Zombies. A troop could walk right up to a Zombie without the fear of being attacked or even seen while he or she would be right in front of a Zombie. The natural defense used synthetically worked like a miracle. This allowed chromosome-protected humans to kill off millions of Zombies in the US alone. Rarely were the humans that were sprayed down losing their lives.

Those deaths too largely were that the Z chromosome's effect didn't last longer than 12-16 hours. Factors such as sweat, humidity, water from rain, or crossing through streams of rivers would eventually wear off the chromosome spray. This knowledge was insightful for humans. Those that were preparing for battle would carry several spray bottles, reapplying to themselves once the magic started wearing off.

Even then, some humans would get blindsided and be bit by a Z. It would hurt, but ultimately it would be a loss for the Z. Since the Z ate any meat, even rotten, when they found one of the warriors dead or dying, they would bite to feed and instantly die. Thousands of Z were dying in this way by biting those that were either alive or were somehow killed.

After receiving the knowledge of the spray's withering effects, those at both Teton and the remaining locations worldwide immediately improved the Z chromosome spray's effectiveness. The light modifications were continually changing, as well. They were discovering other new ways to use these two effective, proven weapons. Novel ideas emerged that devices such as drones and aircraft could employ large spray tanks and release them in heavily populated locations of Zombies and Z.

The satellites being used to track both Zombie and Z helped in this project. Once they discovered target populations, teams would be sent first during the day time to spray the air with crop duster airplanes. Even from high up in the sky, a fleet of Z's could be seen writhing and falling.

With the Z being killed off during the day, the warriors would wait for the sun to set. After that, they would begin the process of tracking down the hideouts of Zombies. The obvious locations were caves and covered buildings and a few houses here and there that provided shelter during the day.

Upon finding these locations, the teams would first set up the lighting at the entry and exit points to keep the Zombies from leaving. Next, teams recently treated with the Z Chromosome would be dispatched. They could enter those locations without being seen though they had to be careful about their steps. After that, there would be simply carnage, mass slaughter of creatures.

On these missions, millions upon millions of Zombies and Z's started to fall. They couldn't defend themselves against these unstoppable attacks. Those who survived were trapped and died of hunger, for they couldn't leave. The lights outside were working at all times, even during the day.

It was an era of celebration for humankind. Soon enough, with the changing of season breeze was starting to roll coldly. Some parts of the country, especially the United States' Northern Region, were experiencing freezing weather again. Teton people knew that the Z's and Zombies would lapse into a winter hibernation like the last time in these areas. But some doubts had begun emerging too.

Chapter 17
The Winter

The leaves started to shed, leaving the branches bare, clad with only thin sheets of snow. Once again, the thicker padded clothes came out, and the condensed fog rolled out of the mouths of the living and the dead alike who breathed.

Like the Winter of 2026, when they had first emerged, the Z and Zombies started retreating into their winter hibernation. This meant that all Z's and Zombies were going into a deep sleep and not actively seeking food sources. If all went according to last year, the scientists at Teton predicted that the creatures would wait until the next Spring when the freezing climate would thaw. They were mobile-only during warmer temperatures.

Teton knew they had to come up with a plan for invading the creatures in the Winter. Some of them were uncertain if the hibernation would happen again as it did last Winter, but confirmation came soon. The creatures that were being monitored were picked up by the satellites. They headed out towards newer hideouts and made preparations for their winter sleep. This only meant that the new plan had to be established very soon. Things were to be up for discussion.

In Teton, all the 11 leaders sat together as they had been sitting for the most pressing concerns lately and reacted about the hibernation. Plans were thrown around the table after everybody was brought on the same page, especially the Wolves, about the creatures' hibernation.

"We have to realize that not all the regions are going to have freezing winters," said one of the former Sheep. There were certain places in the West and along most of the entire Southwest to the Southeast of America with warmer climates that were not going to have freezing temperatures.

"So that means our preparations need to be for selected areas," spoke a Wolf.

"The Northern part of the USA has started experiencing freezing temperatures. If we avail of this opportunity, we can have the chance that we always needed, for completely eradicating the Zombies and Z's. At least the Zombies and Z's that are in the Northern parts can be wiped off entirely," Gus was the one who announced. In exchange, he received several nods.

As the Winter started to break out in places where the tracking devices were all validated, men and women were sent there from Teton. The priority was to kill off all the hibernating Zombies and Z's that they encountered. They didn't have to worry about being attacked by any of the creatures because most of them had fallen into their hibernation already. That, for them, was like being in a deep coma. The warriors knew they would not be able to protect themselves in this state, so some of them moved to the most densely populated areas with Sheep.

For some missions, both survivors and Wolves were transferred. They had had the option of their freedom of choosing what they wanted to do. Would they rather join with Teton, Sheep, and the other Wolves, or would they remain back, not leaving Teton? Some gladly volunteered and joined. Others simply declined and preferred staying back for this one. Most of this latter category were humans that had just returned from war. They wanted to have some time to relax. Though staying back decided to stay near the communication devices to coordinate with those who had traveled out of Teton.

These warriors did promise that "IF you still need our help or assistance, contact us. We will change our minds and join you guys. Just contact us."

These people that decided to stay at home had their stock of both light weapons and also the Z Chromosome spray, just in case. Nobody could be sure about the wildest possibilities coming true. So if Zombies or Z somehow broke into Teton, these people would have to protect themselves. If all goes well, these resting people would have a hibernation of their own, returning next Spring.

At this timeline of earth, every single life was important. It was widely acknowledged that all of humanity had to stay together.

***

The missions started being carried out in the coldest areas in the Northern Part of the United States. The cities and locations that were not secure at this time were going to be made secure. The forces from Teton that had traveled by airplanes and helicopters came to these regions with the same two missions:

The first was to save, help, and rescue any living human they may encounter. Second, to scout and kill all hibernating Zombies and Z's that are in their winter hibernation. They were all going to be defenseless when discovered, so the former Sheep were pretty pleased with carrying out these missions.

The council of 11 back in Teton's rationale was that the cities and locations that had yet to be secured and which were experiencing Freezing temperatures would be the safest places to rebuild human civilization back in America. Any other place had to be on guard because of their climate, but regions, where snow fell, were naturally safer than the rest of the regions. During Winter, the death rates of humans were going to be low due to the Zombies and Z's in deep hibernation.

While snow fell in selected areas, other parts of the country too experienced Winter to some extent. They started to have their own Winter seasonal changes. The Southern Part of America knew that while Zombies and Z's may be slower in the new season, they would still be active and very dangerous.

Rather than battle the Zombies and Z at those remaining warmer locations, mankind thought best that would simply focus on internal survival. They rebuilt themselves and established more order than before. The largest benefit would come by striking in locations that offered little to no resistance to the Zombies and Z's.

Another mission that was still active was finding other Wolves. Some communities had yet to be discovered. Those in Teton had marked some areas, and they had passed the news to correspondents in the free world.

Unlike last Winter, all the efforts in that season were based on working in the areas that were in the stage of early freezing weather. The previous year, Teton's group attempted to also work in the warmer climates that didn't have freezing weather. That action had caused the death of a large percentage of people. That was the rationale behind not indulging the Southern parts in embarking on those missions last Winter. The lesson was learned and would not be repeated.

One group among the scientists had long been looking into the creatures' hibernation due to the cold, freezing weather. For nearly a year, they worked on creating an artificial method of bringing freezing temperatures into other lands on a larger scale. The obvious idea was creating some type of equipment to be used in the places that didn't freeze. Being a season, everyone at Teton knew that eventually, Winter would wear away. Springtime would come again, and humanity may suffer once the Zombies and Z's begin to leave their hibernation cycle again.

The best resolution of all was to kill and destroy as many Zombies and Z that couldn't protect or defend themselves in the just-arrived season.

Earlier, a grand-scale device was thought to prove complications, but A device was indeed finally created. It was similar to a flame thrower, but it would disperse snow-cold frost of sub-zero temperatures at -372 degrees, unlike a flame thrower. Teton was testing this equipment, and reports showed promising results. Against the captured Zombies and Z's that were the test subjects, they worked just as was expected. The movements of the creatures got frozen, and they could do nothing about it.

The weapon earned the name Ice Thrower. It worked with the temperatures that were so much hotter. The ice thrower made them colder than the coldest Winter on earth. Within a millisecond, the ice thrower would instantly freeze what it was being sprayed on. It would become frozen solid.

More than that, the scientists had also predicted that the frozen object, if struck, would even fall to the floor. It was to break into thousands of pieces, and that's just what it did. Not just Zombies and Zs, but even humans and inanimate objects showed the same results if sprayed by the Ice Thrower.

The Ice Thrower came to be tested even outside controlled locations. These new rounds of tests were performed under scorching temperatures. This meant deserts and burning hot cities. The Ice Thrower always proved successful regardless of the weather it was put in. Mother Nature had helped mankind by giving Zombies and Z's cold temperature weaknesses.

The news about the Ice Thrower broke out around the world. It was the third weapon and was exclusively being manufactured only at Teton. The projected deadline for the estimated units would be ready for the springtime against the Zombies and Z's if they would have survived.

These weapons were going to prove fruitful in the upcoming warmer times to come. They were only a few months away.

Since all the Teton missions involved only the coldest of locations, the teams dispatched to those locations did not need artificial lights and other anti-Zombie/Z weapons with them. The Z Chromosome sprays and aerosols were not a major requirement since the Zombies and Z's had been in hibernation. But just to be safe, the warriors always carried those weapons on hand. Nobody knew when chance required them to bring those weapons out in some sudden encounter.

Even while Winter had arrived, Teton and the 19 cities all continued manufacturing these weapons. They hoped for a huge stockpile when it was warmer, and perhaps for also importing to other countries when the time would be right.

Some people who were setting out on missions to the warmer locations kept anti-Zombie and Z weapons.

Time passed away in these preparations until eventually, December 25th arrived that year. There were no more than 1% or those that had comprised the government back in the day. The remaining 1% had long been converted like Gus. The people in charge were the 11 council members in Teton.

It was funny how time had changed all things. Only a year ago, the Wolves were the most hated species by those that once were in charge. This same group led the council (6 out of 11 members) attacks and counter-attacks against the biggest threat to all of humanity: Zombies and Z's. And they had started taking charge in other countries too.

The first time was to recover as many places that were currently freezing eliminate as many Zombies and Z's in these areas as possible. The idea was that one day, the future generations would live in those locations and progress to a healthy, revitalized future. It was predicted to be a future that was going to be better than the present times and the past, led by the 1%. New World Leadership was not going to let the 1% or the former government take control or emerge. They all had done enough harm.

Even if the 1% of the past were alive, they didn't have the experience nor expertise to handle the current world situation had they been given control.

Who could tell if mankind would have even made it this far as they did under Teton 11 and the Wolves? Things were much different this Christmas than in the past. There was unity among men and women working together for all people. Everyone wanted to be rid of the Zombies and Z's. They were now the ultimate threat. Unless they would be eliminated, all of mankind was going to continue to work together.

Even the former Sheep adjusted to the new normal. It wasn't perfect by any means. Their conditioning still bothered them, but it was far superior to how they lived before as Sheep in those former great cities. Cities that were formerly controlled by the 1% with a system of anarchy.

All the cities with Zombies and Z's that were in deep hibernation were being cleared one by one. As soon as they were located, warriors would go in and eliminate the entire clans of Zombies.

Teton continued to grow in numbers while the creatures declined. More and more humans are being found and discovered. In a society ruled by a group of 11, money did not work; the only motivation was collective survival. Everyone contributed, from the oldest to the youngest, all those who could, worked. They cohabited help and made sure that all was taken care of.

Those who were staying back in Teton, along with the council members, felt like on vacation. They were free from the experience of the chaos and carnage as they did last Christmas. Many of them had lived in a warmer climate without any help from Teton last year. These people were the real survivors who discovered and rescued others and set the foundation for a new humanity era. That was something that the Wolves, too, respected.

The Teton people continued to watch and monitor activities in some of the largest cities such as Los Angeles, Phoenix, and Dallas. These were places that were still warm yet had little to no Zombie or Z presence. It was the sign that since the Zombies and Z had begun leaving the cities for food supply, humans in the former metropolis had been becoming extinct and rarely found.

Seeing that, those in Teton then decided to send groups here on missions. These areas had yet to freeze. The mission had to be for gathering supplies, food, clothing, medicine as well as fuel. These cities had plenty of all of these items or so was projected. They just needed to be rummaged through.

"Even more helicopters and military aircrafts may be recovered from these areas if we are lucky," one of the Commander-in-charge addressed the group staying at Teton. These aircraft could be used to transfer back if the supply of items is greater than predicted.

And surely enough, more aircraft were found in these cities. The entire mission was handled most professionally. A total of 16 Helicopters and planes were added to the fleet of aircraft that were in Teton. But this required that more people be trained to fly these aircraft before the onset of Spring. They would then be useful for further scouting missions in projected lands.

Another plan was also to modify all of these aircrafts so that anti-creature lights and Z Chromosome spray could be installed. Lastly, engineers also meant to incorporate the newest weapon, the Ice Thrower. This was a huge undertaking, ensuring humans would not need to fight battles with Zombies and Z's head-on.

The idea of having future battles with the active Zombies and Z's entirely from the sky was most tempting. So many lives could be saved at the expense of nothing but fuel and expert pilots being utilized. Perhaps the traditional attack of land fighting and toe to toe combat could occur only in emergencies. But that was not a huge concern to worry about.

***

After a very productive winter came to an end that practically exterminated all the Zombies and Z's up north, Spring was around the corner again. Zombies and Z's were expected to come out of their deep hibernation. But one thing was sure. This year there would be far lesser Zombies and Z's than last Spring. Man had adapted and prepared better for the fighting that awaited with the remaining Zombies and Z's in the future.

The mistakes of the past were lessons never to be repeated. The most prominent proof for that was that this time, from Washington-Oregon going East to the Illinois area, the entire region, for the most part, was very lowly populated with any remaining Zombies and Z's. Some Zombies and Z's were predictably still there.

The reason was that many in those areas could have been hiding in undiscovered caves and warehouses that were not checked and cleared. Some areas could not be spotted even with drones and satellites, for sometimes power had to be preserved. Even manpower could not suffice for some areas.

The other side to that, the end of Winter marked an era of healing for the Zombies and Z's. If man thought that only man could evolve, he was wrong. These creatures, too, had evolved out of mankind and were not going to go down without a fight.

Out from an underground cave emerged the hallowed and green-skinned figure of a tattered Zombie. It was her first few steps after the Winter. The sun swept away the snow on land, and the only thing that greeted the Zombie was a gentle breeze. With slow, lazy steps, the female Zombie came out, and behind her a flock. The flock increased to team and from team to an army.

No satellite nor drone was spotting them. Had they done so, they could have seen that the tide was turning. By no means was this war over.

ROGER SCHAFER

www.ingramcontent.com/pod-product-compliance
Lightning Source LLC
Chambersburg PA
CBHW031729170626
46808CB00005B/1945